The Angry Horsemen

LEWIS B. PATTEN

Thorndike Press • Thorndike, Maine

Library of Congress Cataloging in Publication Data:

Patten, Lewis B.
   The angry horsemen.

   Originally published: New York : New American Library,
c1960.
   Published in large print.
   1. Large type books. I. Title.
[PS3566.A79A83 1982]   813'.54   82-10534
ISBN 0-89621-383-8

Large Print edition available through arrangement with
The New American Library, Inc.
This novel is a work of fiction. Names, characters, places, and
incidents are either the product of the author's imagination or
are used fictitiously, and any resemblance to actual persons, living or dead, events, or locales is entirely coincidental.

Cover design by Charles C. Cowell.

The
Angry
Horsemen

Chapter One

They rode out of the high country in early October, leaving behind the thickets of pale-trunked golden aspen, the frosty mornings and the cold, clear winds blowing across the top of the world. They began to drop swiftly toward the valley that had looked at first like a pale green thread against the gray background of sage.

Before them traveled the herd, the beef, not as fat this year as last, but still marketable, still very valuable.

Johnny Toothaker could feel a pleasant tension within him, because waiting for him down there was a young woman whom he had married less than three months before. He had been gone three weeks on roundup, and had missed her every hour of every day he had been away.

He turned to Sam Tolle, his partner, riding through a thin fringe of timber a dozen yards away, with a sheepish grin. He called, "You ought to try it, and feel like I feel now."

Sam grinned back mockingly. "Who'd have an old goat like me?" His grin lingered, and warmed, as his eyes rested on Johnny's face. A couple of the hands, riding behind him, began to look at Johnny too and he knew the old, familiar riding was coming.

Johnny took their riding well, in spite of the doubts that hung far back in the recesses of his mind. TT's punchers were more than a crew — they were friends as well.

Arleigh Peters called, "Stop by the henhouse an' pick you up a half a dozen aigs, Johnny. They tell me that's just the thing for old fellers with young ideas."

Jake MacRae chuckled. "Johnny ain't stoppin' fer nothin', are you Johnny?"

The banter went on, good naturedly, and at last Sam Tolle called, while yet a dozen miles from the home place, "Go on in, Johnny. Go on. We don't need you. Your mind ain't even on your work. We'll drop this bunch at three-mile corral and come in later."

Johnny glanced around in embarrassment. Then, reaching the decision suddenly, he touched spurs to his horse, circled the herd

8

and rode ahead. Behind him, Sam Tolle and the others shouted ribald, encouraging jests.

He pushed his horse hard, through a scattering of golden quakie pockets, down long, steep slopes of brush, ochre and dull red with scrub oak and serviceberry bushes.

From behind him, a chill wind knifed out of the high country, giving promise of early winter, and thin clouds scudded swiftly before the sun.

Excitement grew in Johnny as he rode, a tense, pleasant excitement he had never known before — until he met and married Robin. Sam had been wrong — and Sam was seldom wrong — saying it was a mistake for a man to marry a girl half his age.

TT ranch (the TT representing the initials of Toothaker and Toole) lay in a long, wide valley — a high valley that looked south from its lofty perch at the foot of Cottonwood Pass toward the valley of the Blue River, and the snowy peaks of the San Paulo mountains thirty miles beyond.

At sundown, he brought it into sight and looked down hungrily, eagerly, remembering her face clearly now, and her smile — and her warm and laughing eyes.

Deserted, it seemed, except for twin spirals of smoke from the chimneys of bunkhouse and

9

main house. Two or three horses drowsed in the huge pole corral. A couple of milch cows ambled through the creek and up the lane toward the barn.

These three weeks had been worse for her than they had for him, he realized. She wasn't used to loneliness, to the silence of this empty land. She was a city girl, brought up with many people around her, the city's bustle and noise.

Sam Tolle had warned him about that as well as about the difference in their ages. Johnny was forty, Robin only twenty. But they loved each other and that was it.

He angled across the hay meadow, too sparsely dotted this year with brown, fenced stacks of hay, crossed the creek and came up behind the house. He circled it, and tensed to dismount.

He saw her then — saw her come running out of the bunkhouse door. Startled, not yet angry, he saw that her face was flushed, her hair mussed, her dress slightly torn at the throat. She ran toward the house, but stopped and froze, now flushing, as she saw him there astride his horse.

Johnny's eyes, flat with sudden shock, switched from hers, switched to the bunkhouse door. He saw Lou Saks, a young puncher he had left behind to look after things, come running out, out of breath but grinning expectantly.

It didn't take any particular perceptiveness to see what was going on, but it was a couple of long moments before the truth seeped into Johnny's numbed mind. Sam Tolle's warnings — all the ribald jokes — came surging through his mind.

Wildness became like a fire growing in his brain. He flung himself from his horse and crossed the yard toward Lou in a lunging run.

Lou's eyes widened and his face turned gray. He licked his lips, seemed about to speak and then apparently changed his mind.

He was a husky youngster, about Robin's age. Good looking — in a reckless sort of way — he always had a hoard of stories to tell about his conquests. Now he'd be telling this one too — maybe. After Johnny got through with him it would be a while before he'd be talking about anything.

Robin was screaming behind him, "Johnny! Stop it! It's not what you think!"

He wanted to kill then. He hauled himself to a deliberate halt a dozen feet from Lou Saks. He said between clenched teeth, "You dirty son-of-a-bitch! Take pay from me and —"

"I didn't! Damn it Johnny, I swear —"

11

Tall and young and strong, Lou's hair was black and thick, not graying like his own. But he'd show the bastard. He'd show him that being young wasn't everything. He'd beat the living hell out of Lou Saks and then see who Robin thought was the better man.

Resolution came to Lou's eyes as he made the decision to defend himself. And Johnny rushed, swinging.

The blow smashed Lou's lips against his teeth and drove him back. His shoulders struck the bunkhouse wall and a mighty grunt of air whooshed from his lungs.

Johnny followed him, sick and empty inside and knowing only this could bring back his self respect.

Saks hung against the bunkhouse wall for an instant, raised a hand and swiped at his bleeding mouth. He looked at the hand, and then at Johnny. He straightened, something ugly coming into his eyes. He sneered, "Takes a young man to please a woman like that. Takes a man like —"

Johnny rushed, losing all control. Again his fist smashed against Lou's mouth, its force slamming Lou's head back against the weathered logs. Johnny followed that blow with a veritable rain of them — until Lou raised a vicious knee that took him squarely in the crotch.

Pain shot upward like a knife, spreading out through his belly. His head swam. He reeled away.

He staggered and fell, feeling old now, and spent, and helpless before Lou's young strength.

But apparently Lou thought otherwise. Apparently there was considerable respect in him for Johnny's ability to take punishment and bounce right back. Because he didn't come at Johnny with his fists — he seized a pitchfork that was leaning against the bunkhouse wall.

He lunged at Johnny, his knuckles white against the handle of the fork. He drove it down, toward Johnny's chest.

Guilt aimed it there — guilt made him want to kill, just as outraged pride and sensitiveness about his age made Johnny want that too.

Robin screamed, a wordless sound of terror and warning. And Johnny rolled.

The fork plunged into the ground, burying half the length of the tines in the hard, dry surface.

His face white, sweating, his eyes strange and strained with pain, Johnny seized the handle, holding desperately as Saks sought to yank it from the ground.

The fork came free and Saks staggered back, still holding on. Johnny let the fork pull him forward and partly up, knowing he had to hang on because he couldn't dodge again.

Time. He needed time, to recover from the crippling effects of Lou's vicious knee. Time to clear his head, to see again — to feel strength return to his arms and legs.

Lou released the fork suddenly, and Johnny fell back, pulling it with him, pulling it toward himself. Too late, he saw what it would do when he fell.

He struck the ground, and one rusty tine plunged into his thigh. Deep it went, and the pain, on top of the pain he already felt, maddened Johnny and drove the little reason that remained from his mind.

Pain now gave him strength — made him forget that he was hurt and older than his opponent. Pain made him yank out the fork the way a man yanks a snake.

His eyes were not quite sane as he lunged up and forward. Saks saw those eyes and his hand straked for the gun at his side.

Johnny reached him before he could yank it clear. He seized Saks' arms, the one holding the gun, and half turned, bringing it down hard across his raising knee.

It cracked dully as it broke, and a high, thin sound escaped Saks' lips. The gun dropped from his crippled fingers.

Johnny flung him furiously away. Saks fell on the broken arm, and a scream like a woman's tore from his twisted, saliva-flecked lips. Consciousness left him and he lay still, as though he were dead.

Johnny glared down at him, unsatisfied, feeling stronger now and wishing there had been more fight in Saks. He heard a sound from Robin, and switched his glance to her. He panted shortly, angrily, "Go to the house. I'll take care of you later."

Her eyes sparkled with anger. "You'll take care of me later? For what? Just what do you think I've done?"

"Pretty plain, ain't it? He didn't drag you into the bunkhouse, did he?"

She flushed at that and her glance wavered. She studied his face uncertainly for a moment, and her youth showed now.

She was a small-bodied, but strong girl, wearing today a checked blue gingham dress. Her hair, which unpinned came to her waist, was like black silk, but it had a brownish cast rather than a bluish one. Her eyes, normally soft, were angry, and hurt, and beginning to sparkle with tears. Johnny looked away from them deliberately and strode across the yard toward the pump.

He picked up a rusty bucket and pumped it

full. It leaked like a sieve, but he carried it across the yard and dumped it on Lou's head.

Sputtering, the man rolled. Without sitting up, he stared at Johnny's face.

Johnny said, "Get out of here and don't come back. Get clear out of the country. If I see your face in Cottonwood, I'll blow your brains out."

"You owe me —"

Johnny's voice was like ice. "Don't tell me what I owe you! I might pay it off! Get your pay from Tolle when he gets here. But don't let me see your face again."

"You can't do this!" His voice wavered and died. He cleared his throat and struggled to sit up. His face twisted with pain and sweat sprang out anew on his forehead. He growled, "Winter's comin', an' jobs are scarce."

"You should have thought of that before." Johnny stared at him angrily.

Lou said defiantly, "I'll tell —"

Johnny kicked him, fighting himself, hating himself because with that kick he was trying to silence not only Lou, but a voice within himself as well.

It could never be the same again, that voice told him. He could never wholly trust her again. He swung around and headed for the house. The corner of his eye caught the move-

16

ment of horsemen coming out of the creek behind the house.

Sam Tolle and the roundup crew. There would be no hiding what had happened from them.

Johnny wanted to run. He didn't want to face them now. But he stood rooted to the ground, staring toward their approaching shapes defiantly.

Sam Tolle was fifty, heavy-set and grizzled. Tough and hard, he had big-brothered Johnny since the time, twenty-five years before, when he'd picked Johnny off a freight and begun to teach him the cattle business. Now his wise, ice-blue eyes took in all that had happened instantly.

He looked at Robin, not unkindly, and said, "Go in the house, girl. We'll talk later."

For an instant, Robin seemed about to speak. Then, without doing so, she turned and ran into the house.

Sam glanced at Johnny, then around at the crew. "Take Saks into the bunkhouse and splint his arm. A couple of you hitch up a buckboard to take him to town. Throw some hay in the back."

They dismounted and moved to obey his orders, their glances touching Johnny furtively. Sam walked out into the middle of the yard, beckoning Johnny to follow. Johnny limped after him. He could feel the blood trickling down his thigh from the pitchfork wound. He'd have to have it opened up, and soon. A pitchfork wound could make a man lose his leg if it wasn't taken care of immediately.

Sam asked, "What happened?"

Johnny glared at him. "My business. I don't want to talk about it. Give Lou his pay and get him out of here."

Sam said, "Did anything happen? Or did you jump to a bunch of conclusions? I know Robin and I don't think —"

"She was comin' out of the bunkhouse door with Saks chasin' her." The words came out surlily, reluctantly, and after he had uttered them Johnny didn't like himself much.

"I didn't have to. I got eyes, haven't I?"

"Hadn't you better hear her side of it?"

Johnny stared at him furiously. "Whose side you on, anyhow, hers or mine? Goddam it, any woman knows better than to go bargin' in the bunkhouse. She don't do it unless she's lookin' for something."

"She's a city girl. She's been alone three weeks. Maybe she didn't mean no harm."

Johnny felt an unreasonable, rising anger. He stared at Sam, suddenly not liking him at all. He growled, "To hell with you — and her too. I'm going to town and get Doc to look at this leg."

"What happened to it?"

"None of your goddam business!" Johnny whirled and, trying not to limp, walked to his horse, standing groundtied a dozen yards away. Without looking at Sam, he swung to the saddle. He spurred cruelly and thundered out of the yard, south toward the town of Cottonwood, fifteen miles away.

Something within him, some deep conscience or shame, told him he was acting childishly, and he knew that if Tolle hadn't defended Robin, if he had condemned her instead, Johnny's attitude would have been vastly different.

But something else kept prodding him — his own deep worry that Sam had been right all along. Maybe it had been a mistake to marry Robin. He was twice her age. And if this had happened so soon after their marriage, might it not happen again?

He raked his weary horse with his spurs and the animal lunged into a reckless run. But Johnny couldn't run away from his thoughts, no matter how he tried.

Chapter Two

As he rode, the gray light of dusk faded slowly from the sky. Looking up at the first bright stars winking out, he tried not to think how different things had been an hour ago. He had been hurrying home to her, eager and excited as a boy. And now —

Damn her! Damn! He remembered again the way she had looked standing out there in the yard. A kind of ache came to his chest, an ache of hunger, and disappointment and frustration.

He should never have married her, but he had, and now by God he'd see to it that she behaved herself. If he had to fire every damn man on the ranch.

He scowled, and became aware that his horse was faltering. It was full dark now, and he let up on the animal, let him drop back to a plodding walk.

The injured thigh was a steady, maddening ache of pain that drove reasonableness from his mind. What the hell had she been doing in the bunkhouse anyway? Didn't she know that was a place no woman went?

Fire every man on the ranch, every one young enough to interest her or be interested in her. And what then? Lock her in a room? He gritted his teeth helplessly.

Maybe he ought to send her away – back to Denver. Maybe he ought to divorce her.

The thought was like a knife stabbing him. He couldn't let her go, couldn't give her up. He'd given her a part of himself when he married her, a part he'd never given anyone else in his whole life before. She'd take that part of him with her if she went away.

She had been running – *away* from Saks. She hadn't been laughing, either, to invite pursuit. Maybe it *had* been innocent. She was young. She could make a mistake. Maybe Saks had mistaken loneliness and friendliness for something else.

He wanted suddenly to turn around and go back – hear her side of it – straighten it out and apologize to her if he had been in the wrong.

His horse put a foot into a washout crossing the road and lurched. Johnny jarred forward, against the pommel of the saddle. The pitchfork wound sent sudden, maddening waves of pain up his thigh and into his groin —

And the need to turn back was gone. Fury soared in his mind again. He hated Saks, hated Sam Tolle, hated Robin too. He spurred his horse and forced the weary animal into a rolling lope.

This way, at eight, he came into the town of Cottonwood.

It lay at the foot of the long, steep road leading north to the summit of Cottonwood Pass, and passing TT on the way. You came into it suddenly, from an altitude of a hundred or more feet above it, and could look down and see each house and each twinkling light.

Usually, even after all these years, seeing it thus gave Johnny a little thrill of pleasure. Tonight it did not. He reined his horse around the steep bend at the top of the hill and put him into the road leading down.

Doc Peabody's office was over the Boggs Bank, but Johnny knew he wouldn't be there tonight. So, when he reached the foot of the hill and entered the town, he turned right on Cedar Street and headed straight for Doc's house.

It was dark, empty, which did not tend to improve Johnny's disposition. It had been a long ride and pain had been a constant companion.

He swung around and rode toward the center of town. Doc was probably on the veranda of the Buckhorn Hotel, swapping stories with some of the oldsters loafing there.

The main street in Cottonwood was Cottonwood Avenue, and it held the hotel, three saloons and most of the other businesses of the town except for the livery barns and blacksmith shop. The hotel dominated the intersection of Cottonwood and River, with the bank diagonally across.

Several men called out to Johnny as he rode down the center of the street, their tones friendly. Johnny Toothaker was almost universally liked in Cottonwood.

But tonight he gave them no response. Sitting like a lump in his saddle, he reined up before the hotel veranda and stared down at Doc, on the steps with Len Purdue.

He said, "Want you to look at my leg, Doc. I ran a pitchfork into it." He fought himself, sitting there, fought the rising irritability that struggled to express itself in his voice.

Doc got up. Purdue cackled, "Whatsa matter,

23

Johnny? That new wife take to you with a pitchfork?"

Johnny glared at him.

Doc stepped down into the street and headed across toward his office over the bank. Purdue kept cackling and muttering something to himself. Johnny wanted to go back and bust him in the mouth. He clenched his hands.

What was the matter with him? This wasn't the first time Len Purdue had kidded him about Robin, and some of Len's jokes got pretty raw. Always before Johnny had taken them good-naturedly, knowing that was the way they were offered.

Tonight, though, the humor was gone from him. Tonight he wanted to hit something, pound something with his fists.

Doc climbed the outside stairs and unlocked the door. Johnny limped after him. Inside, Doc lighted a lamp and trimmed the wick.

Doc was a short, untidy man who wore a blue serge suit, shiny from wear in the seat of the pants and at the elbows. There was gravy or something on one lapel and on his tie. He wore black, high shoes with a round, bull-dog toe, and they probably hadn't been shined for weeks.

He said gruffly, "Well, don't just stand there. Take off your pants."

24

Johnny unbuckled his gun and hung it on the back of a chair. He sat down, wincing as he did, and pulled off his boots. Then he took off his pants.

Dock said, "Get that damn underwear off too, unless you want me to cut it."

Johnny said grumpily, "Go ahead and cut it."

"Lie down on the couch."

Johnny lay down. His temper was wearing thin.

Doc slit the underwear and looked at the wound, now a bluish spot that wasn't bleeding at all. "How deep did it go?"

"Couple inches I suppose."

"Covered with manure and rust, too, I'll bet."

"Probably."

"I'll have to lance it."

"All right. Go ahead."

Doc crossed the room to his desk. He got out a fresh brown bottle of whisky and pulled the cork. "Drink about half of this."

Johnny took a long pull at the bottle. Doc kept examining the wound. He glanced up, grinning faintly. "Couple inches more to the right and you wouldn't of been much bridegroom. You'd a had to leave them chores to the younger men."

Johnny felt raw fury soar in his brain.

"You lecherous old bastard, shut your mouth. Before I shut it for you."

Doc stared at him, the grin fading. His eyes turned hard. "What the hell are you so damn mean for? You been hurt before — worse than this."

Johnny said, "Just shut your mouth and do what you're gettin' paid to do."

Doc whistled soundlessly, his eyes still hard as stone. "I'll get paid all right. The bill I send TT for this will be a whopper."

Johnny clenched his jaws. It didn't help his frame of mind to fight with Doc. He was sorry he'd been so nasty, but he couldn't bring himself to say he was sorry. Doc had probed a mighty sore place with that crack of his about younger men.

Doc said testily, "Drink that damn whisky so I can get this over with."

Johnny drank. The whisky almost gagged him, but he forced it down. His head began to whirl. He lay back and stared with brooding eyes at the ceiling.

Doc worked in silence, sponging off the leg with alcohol, packing towels around it to catch the expected flow of blood.

He said as he picked up his surgical knife, "Hold onto something. This'll hurt like hell."

Johnny grabbed the rails of the couch at his sides.

He felt the knife go in. The yell broke from his lips involuntarily. He tightened his grip on the rails of the couch and felt them bend. Then, mercifully, he lost consciousness.

When he came to, several minutes later, Doc was just finishing putting on the bandage. Johnny felt weak, and sick.

Doc finished and Johnny sat up. Doc pushed him back. "Lay there a while. You got nothin' else to do." He grinned at Johnny maliciously. "You won't be doin' any stud-horsin' for a spell."

The remark, innocent enough, brought back to Johnny the memory of his fight with Lou Saks and the reasons for it.

He sat up and dropped his legs over the side of the couch. Pain shot upward from the wound in his thigh. Sweat sprang out in beads on his forehead.

There was a bulky white bandage around his thigh. The leg of his underwear was cut clear off and had slipped down around his ankle.

He pulled it off and flung it into a corner. He got up, fighting dizziness, and reached for his pants. Leaning against the wall, he put them on, then sat down on the couch and put on his boots.

Doc watched him, his eyes curious and puzzled and still a little angry. He said, as Johnny buckled on his gun, "How'd you manage to run a pitchfork into you? I thought you were out on roundup."

Johnny glared at him without answering. Doc's face grew red. He grumbled, "Well to hell with you! Keep it to yourself, if that's the way you feel about it!"

Johnny stalked out of the office, clumped down the stairs to the street. The hard core of anger and irritability still lingered in him, aggravated by pain, which had now spread to emcompass his whole leg. But there was something else in him now as well — puzzlement. Always before there had been a closeness and comraderie between himself and Doc Peabody he'd thought nothing could shake or destroy. Yet it had been destroyed by a moment of anger and a few harsh words. It had been shattered by an unthinking jest, one that struck hard and deep at a worry already rooted in Johnny's mind.

At the foot of the steps he halted, trying hard to get a grip on himself. He had to go home. He had to face Robin. Somehow he had to kill the jealousy and self-doubt eating at him and face her with an open mind.

Maybe a drink or two would help. Maybe it

would relax his mind and stop the angry, jealous thoughts that kept churning in it. Shock and pain had already killed the effects of Doc's whisky.

He turned and limped along downstreet in the direction of the Stag Saloon.

Passing the lighted windows of Berkely's Mercantile, he saw a boy trot from behind it, carrying a .22 rifle and two rabbits. Jess Morey's boy. The boy saw Johnny, grinned widely and called, holding the rabbits, "Hi, Johnny. Look what I got."

Johnny said, "Pretty good. Fine," but there was no enthusiasm in his voice. The boy shot him a puzzled stare and crossed the dark street, disappearing from sight between two buildings on the far side. Johnny scowled at the place he had disappeared, thinking.

TT ranch occupied a peculiar position in the lives of the people of Cottonwood and the surrounding area. Monstrously large, it might have earned their resentment and even their hatred if it had been operated differently.

It controlled the route leading to the high country dominated by Cottonwood Pass. It controlled the water of Cottonwood Creek, flowing down through the lower valley ranches. It owned the winter range at the lower elevations and it raised virtually all the hay used by the country's cattlemen and sold them what they needed every fall at somewhat less than the going price.

Sam Tolle always said, "Man's a fool that don't try to get along with his neighbors. It don't pay to think you're so goddam big you don't need 'em." And so, the policy of TT ranch had been to release water to the lower valley ranches when they needed it, to allow them use of TT's winter range, to run their cattle with TT's herd in the high country during summer. Johnny and Sam and the roundup crew had gathered, in addition to their own cattle, cattle belonging to nine others, ranging in numbers from Jess Morey's seven head to Hank Stoner's three hundred.

Johnny heard the rattle of a buckboard behind him and swung around. The buckboard stopped at the foot of the stairs leading up to Doc Peabody's office just as the light went out upstairs.

He heard Doc's door close at the head of the stairs, heard Arleigh Peters shout from the buckboard, "Wait a minute, Doc. I got a patient for you."

He heard Doc's voice, "What'd you have up there, a fight?"

The answer was indistinguishable, but consisted of several sentences, at the end of which Peters laughed. There was more talk, and then Johnny heard, "– Lou Saks – broken arm."

Doc said, "Bring him up," and a moment later his light went on again, brightened as he lowered the chimney over the wick.

Johnny's face was hot. Big joke! The story of that fight would be all over town in another hour, all over the country by morning.

Fury burned in his heart, thinking of it. Damn them! Damn them all!

And yet, a little stir of doubt was born in the back of his mind. What if he'd been wrong? What if Robin *had* gone to the bunkhouse only because she was lonely and didn't know better? What if it had only been a case of Lou misunderstanding and making unwelcome advances?

By the time the story got through making the rounds, Robin's reputation would be ruined. Half the women in the country were jealous of her anyway; they thought Johnny should have married a local girl. Johnny knew from past experience how spiteful their gossip could get.

He kicked out savagely at a tin can laying on the walk – and winced at the pain. The can rolled noisily into the street.

With his face set, his eyes smoldering, Johnny stalked purposefully along toward the doors of the saloon.

31

Chapter Three

Sam Tolle watched Johnny ride out of the yard. He glanced uncertainly toward the house, then around toward the bunkhouse door, where Arleigh Peters had just halted the buckboard. There was a foot of hay in the buckboard. A couple of the others helped Saks in.

He sat, holding his broken arm steady with the other hand. His face was pale, his eyes angry.

Tolle had no sympathy for him. A man that didn't have any better sense than to try for the boss's wife deserved anything that happened to him.

Tolle took three tens out of the currency in his wallet and crossed to the buckboard. He handed them to Saks without speaking. Saks took them and tucked them down in his shirt pocket.

Arleigh Peters spoke to the horses and the buckboard rattled out of the yard. Peters wasn't driving either slowly or carefully, and this told Tolle better than anything could have told him that the men had no more sympathy for Saks than he had.

Reluctantly, he walked toward the house, feeling very old tonight. Johnny was too hotheaded, but Sam guessed he couldn't blame him much. Johnny was forty years old and had been single all his life. He hadn't quite believed his good fortune when Robin had agreed to marry him, so it wasn't surprising now that he was ready to believe the worst.

Sam hadn't helped Johnny either by expressing doubts as to the wisdom of the match. He had, without really intending to, planted doubts in Johnny's mind — about his age in relation to Robin's, and the chances for success in such a marriage. Now those doubts were taking solid shape. And no telling what they'd make Johnny do.

Sam hoped Lou Saks would take Johnny's advice and get out of the country. Because if he didn't, he could cause one hell of a lot of trouble.

It had been a hot, dry year anyhow. There wasn't enough hay to sell the lower valley ranchers that needed it. And they'd need more than usual this year because water had been short all summer and they hadn't raised as much themselves as they usually did.

So far things were harmonious enough, though Sam had detected a strained quality in the cordiality of those who depended upon TT. Nor was this new complication going to help. Johnny had always come in for a lot of kidding about Robin, which he'd taken surprisingly well. Now – he'd flare up at anybody that made a remark about his age and ability as a husband. And those he flared at were likely to flare right back. Frowning, Sam went into the house.

Robin sat huddled at one end of a monstrous cowhide-covered sofa. She glanced up, her face streaked with tears.

Sam crossed to her. She was a pretty thing, he thought. But too much of a child for a mature man like Johnny. He sat down beside her and patted her shoulder awkwardly.

She covered her face and sobbed brokenly. After a while she wiped the tears from her eyes with the back of a slender hand and turned to look at him. "I didn't mean any harm, Sam."

"Didn't figure you did."

"I was just lonesome. I thought if I didn't talk

34

to someone I'd go crazy. So I went out to the bunkhouse to talk to Lou."

"That's what I figured."

"But not what Johnny figured." Her face flushed slightly with anger and her eyes sparkled.

Sam said patiently, "Johnny's got a chip on his shoulder about his age. Since you two got married, the whole country has kidded him about it. I didn't help any either, I guess. Before you got married, I told him he was taking an awful chance."

Her eyes fell away from his. After a moment she asked, "Was Johnny hurt badly?"

"Pitchfork tine in the thigh. He went to town to have Doc Peabody lance it."

She shivered slightly in sympathy for Johnny's pain. "And it's all my fault." Her eyes lifted and stubbornly clung to Sam's. "I'm going to be honest. I *did* like Lou. I couldn't help thinking about him sometimes."

Sam could tell it was hard for her to meet his steady glance. But she didn't let her eyes waver. "I'll tell Johnny that. If I'm truthful—"

Sam shook his head, with amazement and unbelief. "For God's sake, whatever you do, don't tell him that! Who's it going to help? You? It sure as hell won't help Johnny. It'll just convince him that he was right all the time."

35

She colored painfully. "I'm afraid he was."

"You mean you *wanted* Lou to – make love to you?"

"Oh no! But I did flirt with him a little. I felt so – so *drab!* And I missed Johnny. Oh, I don't know, Sam. I don't!"

Sam grinned. "Don't take yourself so blasted serious. Everyone that's married looks around a little now and then. Thing to do is forget it. Just let Johnny know you're in love with him. Make him feel young and important. And above all, walk the straight and narrow. No flirting. Don't even talk to another man." His grin widened. "Except me, of course."

"You're sure it isn't too late?"

"Johnny's crazy about you. He won't let you go."

"Do you think he'll come back tonight?"

Sam shrugged. "I don't know. If he doesn't come back by midnight, I'll ride into town."

Robin stared at him. Her eyes were soft, troubled. She was very pale. "Am I good for him, Sam? Can I ever make him a good wife? I'm so green! I do things without thinking about the consequences. Like today."

Sam grinned ruefully. "You think you're the only one who does that? I'll bet that right now Johnny is doing exactly the same thing." The grin faded and his eyes grew worried. "I just hope he doesn't start something he can't finish. Things are touchy right now anyhow, what with everybody short of hay and winter range."

He gave her back a reassuring, final pat and stood up, thinking it was hell to be young, thinking too that he wouldn't go back and be young again for anybody. You didn't know the rules, and no matter how you tried, you kept making disastrous mistakes. Like Robin's — like the one Johnny had made in kicking up such a fuss with Lou before he even knew what had happened.

A peculiar feeling of uneasiness began to trouble him. He knew Johnny — knew that in spite of Johnny's forty years the juices of youth still flowed in him. Usually easygoing, Johnny had a temper that sometimes ran wild and virtually impossible to control. If those he met in town tonight chose to renew their corny jokes about his age and Robin's youth—

Sam went out of the house. He walked across the yard aimlessly, puzzling at the broody, troubled feeling that possessed him. Hell, nothing was going to happen. Johnny might snap back at someone, or he might even get into another fight. But that was about the worst of it. Unless the fight were one with guns.

Suddenly, impulsively, he strode toward the corral. Johnny was alone in town, hurt, angry, jealous and uncertain. If he ever needed support, he needed it now. Sam roped out a horse, saddled, and galloped away toward town, hoping he was not already too late.

Lou Saks endured the jolting ride to town with gritted teeth and pale and sweating face. A couple of times he felt himself slipping away into unconsciousness, but both times he held on grimly and stubbornly until the moment passed.

He thought of Johnny Toothaker — thought of what he would do to Johnny when this damned arm healed. Hell, there hadn't been any call for Johnny to get that rough. What Lou had done was only what any man would do. That fancy piece of Johnny's had come barging into the bunkhouse just like she wanted Lou to try for her. Only when he had, she'd gotten scared, and run away. It was Lou's tough luck that Johnny had picked that particular moment to ride into the yard.

Damn a woman like that anyhow. They smiled at you; they hunted you out and made talk; they flirted with their eyes and words. But when you took them up on it they folded like a poker player with a busted flush. Teasers.

And this one had made him lose a job, and made him get this busted arm so that even if he could locate another job he couldn't hold it. How the hell was a man suppose to feed cattle, do chores, even ride in winter with a busted arm?

The bitter truth was that he faced the coming winter with thirty dollars and no prospects of getting more.

And by God, TT ought to pay. Johnny Toothaker ought to pay!

A spare, humorless smile touched Lou's mouth. Thing to do was to see to it that they did. Maybe this winter wouldn't turn out so bad after all. If Lou was smart, it *could* turn out real well.

Arleigh Peters wheeled the buckboard into the turn at the top of the hill north of town with reckless disregard for Lou's comfort. He whipped the horses up and bounded down the hill, taking corners with sliding wheels. Lou Saks stared at his back with open hatred.

They all stuck together. Peters was foreman, second only to the partners. Toothaker and Tolle. Like Johnny, Peters figured Lou was in the wrong, that he'd tried to force himself on Robin. So he was going to see to it that this ride was just as painful and uncomfortable as he could possibly make it for Lou.

Lou's lips moved soundlessly, "You too, you son-of-a-bitch! I'll get you after I'm through with Johnny."

Peters pulled up in front of Doc's office and Lou was thrown forward against the seat. Peters yelled up to Doc, who was just closing his door up there on the landing. "Wait a minute, Doc. I got a patient for you."

Doc and Peters yelled back and forth. Peters made no move to help Lou out of the buckboard. At last Lou grabbed the edge with his left hand and vaulted out by himself.

The jolt as he struck the board sidewalk sent shock waves of pain all the way up his arm. His head grew light. The glowing flame of hatred leaped a little higher.

Peters didn't offer to help him up the stairs, so Lou stubbornly began to fight his way up them by himself.

His lips moved soundlessly. His eyes were virulent.

Doc went back inside, lighted a lamp and trimmed the wick. Lou staggered into his untidy, musty-smelling office and collapsed into a chair, Doc stared at him, disapproval plain in his face. Lou stared back with open hatred.

Speaking to Arleigh Peters, Doc said, "I take it there was a fight up there. Johnny was in a while ago to have me lance a pitchfork wound. What was it all about?"

Peters stared briefly at Lou. He was a stocky, oldish man with cold blue eyes and a thin, uncompromising mouth. He said with a bit of reluctance, "Guess you'll hear it anyhow. Johnny rode in from roundup and found his wife running out of the bunkhouse with this bastard after her. He lost his head."

Doc whistled softly. "Can't say I blame him."

Peters said hastily, "She's a good woman, Doc. She's young and she was raised in the city, but she's a good woman an' anyone that says she ain't has got me to fight. I got an idea she was lonesome and only wanted to talk, but this bastard—"

Lou said angrily, "Goddam it, why blame it all on me? She—"

The eyes of both Peters and Doc were like ice on a winter stream. Peters said ominously, "Shut your filthy mouth before I shut it for you."

Lou grumbled, "Doc, you goin' to set this arm or not?"

Doc said, "I'll set it." He came over to Lou and began to remove the temporary splints put on by the TT crew. His hands were deft, but it was plain from his eyes that he wanted to hurt Lou. It was also plain from his manner that he was stubbornly resisting the compulsion.

Even so, the pain was excruciating. Sweat

41

popped out on Lou's forehead. Weakness and dizziness swept over him in waves.

Fortunately the fracture was a simple one, and relatively simple to set. Once Lou growled, "Do a good job, damn you, or I'll make you wish you had. That's my work arm."

"Gun arm, I suppose," sneered Peters. "Take my advice and clear out of the country like Johnny told you to. You stay around, and you'll wind up dead."

"Or he will!"

Peters' expression became suddenly very bland, very dangerous. "You threatening him?"

"Maybe. By God, maybe I am. What you goin' to do about it, shoot me down right here? Or beat me up with your fists?" There was no fear in Lou. He was maddened by the pain in his arm, which Doc was now binding up. He didn't care what Peters did.

Doc interrupted, "You keep this arm still. If you don't, you'll slip the ends of the bones and the arm won't heal right."

Lou stared up at him. "It better heal right, Doc. It just better."

Peters smiled grimly, contemptuously. "He's full of threats tonight."

Lou didn't reply. But his mind said, "Maybe they ain't threats, you son-of-a-bitch! Maybe they ain't threats at all. TT's been throwin' its weight around this country just about long enough. Maybe it's time somebody did somethin' about it. An' that somebody might turn out to be me!"

He got up and stalked to the door. Peters called after him, "You got forty-eight hours. When it's up, you'd better be gone."

Lou turned and stared at him venomously. Then, walking gingerly, he made his way down the outside stairs. All he could think was that somehow, he was going to get even with them all. If it killed him.

Chapter Four

Limping painfully and lightheaded from loss of blood, Johnny Toothaker pushed aside the doors of the Stag Saloon and stepped inside.

The liquor Doc had made him drink was now having a delayed effect upon him, adding to his already foul mood a quality of recklessness. His head felt as though there were pressure in it, and every now and then, when his thoughts returned to Robin, his mouth would tighten ominously.

He limped across the sawdust floor to the bar. He nodded at Lewt Rhea, the bartender, and Lewt slid him a bottle and glass.

Johnny stood at the bar, tall, graying at the temples but hard and tough and competent. At forty, he owned half of a hundred thousand dollar ranch, and granted that Sam Tolle had taught him the cattle business, he'd done his share and more in building it.

Johnny was the mover of the partnership, the one who drove himself and others until the job, whatever it was, was done. Sam was the one who smoothed the feathers Johnny sometimes ruffled. Sam was the business manager, more patient and tolerant.

Sensitive about his age for the first time in his life, Johnny was so now only because of Robin. Actually he was in the prime of his life, physically and mentally too. He was range bull, all male, all driving virility. He had overwhelmed Robin, had virtually taken her breath away. Having married him, she found that he made love just as he did everything else, in a direct, driving, ruthless way that brooked no protest, indeed heard none. She liked it, too, because it made her feel as much woman as Johnny was man.

Johnny downed his first drink and grimaced almost imperceptibly at its taste. He felt an elbow dig him in the ribs, felt pain shoot from his hurt leg because of it. He swung his head.

Nathan Dunn stood beside him, grinning in a friendly, mocking way. He said in a sly, suggestive voice, "Wondered how long it would take."

"How long what would take?" Dunn didn't

seem to notice Johnny's eyes, which were edgy and hard.

"For her to wear you out. You're too damned old for a young woman like her, Johnny. But then hell, that's what good neighbors are for."

Johnny asked evenly, "You a good neighbor, Dunn?"

Dunn caught his tone. Puzzlement and concern touched his eyes. "Don't get riled, Johnny. I didn't mean nothin'. I just wanted to ask you about them three stacks of hay down against my fence. I was up the other day, but you weren't at home. Hope nobody else has spoke for 'em yet."

"You were up the other day?"

"Sure." Dunn studied Johnny with puzzled eyes. "What's wrong with that?"

Johnny mimicked. "I don't know. What *is* wrong with that? Supposing you tell me."

Dunn muttered uneasily, "Somethin's happened. Maybe I'd better come up and see you tomorrow."

Johnny said flatly, "Not tomorrow or any other goddam day. You don't get the hay. We need it."

"Johnny, I—"

"I said you didn't get the hay, didn't I? You got ears, haven't you?"

"All right, Johnny." Dunn's tone was placating, as though with a drunk. It only served to infuriate Johnny further.

He wanted to hit Nate Dunn. He wanted to rage at him, to curse him. He turned away deliberately and stared at the bottle before him. The knuckles of his hands, gripping the edge of the bar, were white with strain.

Muttering unintelligibly, Nate Dunn backed away. He turned and hurried from the saloon.

Johnny didn't particularly like himself right then. Nate Dunn was a friend, and TT had always let him buy the hay down near his fence. Johnny knew Dunn had to have it, or sell his herd.

Compromises were going to have to be made because TT was desperately short of hay this year themselves. But that didn't mean they were going to stop helping their neighbors.

Standing there moodily, Johnny took a long, slow look at himself and didn't like what he saw. Jealousy was, he realized, a terrible thing. It had changed him, in a matter of hours, from a competent, if driving, man into a bad-tempered bastard who lashed out at everyone he saw.

And his jealousy was compounded by self-doubt and sensitiveness about his age in relation to Robin's. But he couldn't help himself. Knowing the cause of his viciousness, he was nevertheless unable to stop it. Every time he thought of Robin, he saw her face, flushed with both excitement and guilt, saw her mussed hair, the torn neckline of her dress — and his fury rose.

Outside in the street, Nate Dunn paused to shape a cigarette from the brown papers and sack of Bull Durham he carried in his vest. His eyes were burning — furious — but they were scared and worried too.

TT had always sold him hay. He depended on it. Maybe it had been a mistake — it looked so now — but he'd bought more cattle than he could possibly feed with the hay he grew himself. Damn Johnny anyway! Johnny knew refusing him hay meant he'd have to sell them off. This year he'd hardly raised enough hay himself to winter his horses and three milch cows.

Johnny knew something else too. Most of Nate's herd was composed of young cows and calves. With the market the way it was he couldn't realize more than half of what he had in them.

Nate was a big man, outwardly slow and methodical. He had a wife inclined to thinness and sharpness, and three children, the youngest of whom was seven and the oldest, Will, fifteen.

Nate's father had, all his life, worn his pride like a suit of armor, boasting that he accepted favors from no man. As a boy, Nate had often disagreed with such stiff-necked pride, but it had, nevertheless, left its mark on him.

Taking so much from TT seemed like a betrayal of his father's principles, and made him feel like a failure. As a consequence, he resented TT bitterly, indeed sometimes even hated them.

It was for his children that Nate Dunn worked and built. It was for them he accepted TT's favors. His father's eternal pride had resulted in unnecessary privation and hardship for his family. Nate was determined that such would not be the case with him.

But now, if he sold that herd, he'd be right back where he started eight years ago and wouldn't even have his pride.

The thought turned him desperate. Will was already fifteen. Starvation and poverty wouldn't keep him home.

Will liked cattle work and had done a man's work all summer, riding with the TT crew as his share of the work connected with TT's pasturing his father's herd. Owning cattle, working with them, made Will feel big and important. He wouldn't like selling off the cattle any more than Nate did. And he wouldn't stay around home with the cattle gone. He'd run away, just as Nate himself had at fifteen.

Nate scowled savagely. Johnny's behavior continued to puzzle him because it wasn't like Johnny. Or maybe, by God, it was. Maybe this was the real Johnny, and the one Nate had become used to was only a sham, a fake.

He'd see Sam Tolle – but then he shook his head. Sam was Johnny's partner. He'd back up anything Johnny did. He had to.

With a sudden, angry movement, Nate flung his cigarette into the street and crossed toward the Boar's Head. Furious resentment smoldered in him. That was the trouble with accepting favors – you never knew when they'd be cut off. His father had been right. A man ought to live by his own toil and sweat, accepting nothing from anyone. That way, you knew what to expect. Nobody else could cut the ground out from under you.

How the hell was he going to tell his wife, and Will, that he'd get no hay from TT this year? He considered only briefly trying to persuade Johnny to reverse his decision, or appealing to Sam Tolle. He wouldn't beg! Damn it, he wouldn't do that – not if he starved!

Damn them anyway! He'd done a sight more

than any of TT's other neighbors. He'd insisted on having Will ride with them all summer as payment for summer graze. And he'd consistently paid the going price for TT's hay, even once or twice when Sam Tolle offered it to him for less.

And so his fury smoldered and grew. He slammed into the Boar's Head and clumped angrily across to the bar, muttering to himself, "Goddam sons-of-bitches! Get a man dependin' on 'em, and then spring the trap. Like as not the bastards are just doin' this so's they can pick up my cattle from me cheap!"

He ordered a drink and downed it at a gulp. He poured another and downed that too. He poured a third and it followed the others in quick succession, but the third one gagged him and he made a face.

For a while he stood there, staring broodingly at the brown bottle before him. Then he heard a commotion behind him and turned.

The liquor, consumed so fast, had gone quickly to his head. He wasn't used to drinking much and he'd had more tonight than ever before at one time.

Lou Saks, one of TT's punchers, had come in and had gravitated immediately to Whitey Post and another known only as Kiowa, from over at the foot of the San Paulo range. The pair had no ranch, and no visible means of support, but they always seemed to have money.

Lou was loud and half drunk. His arm was in a sling, and his eyes were evidence of the pain he was suffering. He was cursing TT and particularly Johnny Toothaker and apparently didn't care who heard.

"The son of a bitch! Him an' that fancy piece he married! I'll kill him. That's what I'll do. I'll kill him!"

Kiowa, a dark-haired, dark-skinned man with a cold, impassive face, murmured something and Lou shouted, "What happened? I'll tell you what happened! That goddam wife of his came smellin' around the bunkhouse today while he was gone. She teased around a while and finally I took her up on it. She ran like hell and Johnny had to pick that particular time to come ridin' into the yard. I run a pitchfork into him an' he broke my arm. Then he fired me. Me! When what he ought to of done was beat the hell out of her. Christ, what's a man supposed to do, push a good-lookin' one like her away?"

Whitey said, "You'd have been better off if you had."

Lou glared at him. "Maybe not. Maybe I'll just be a sight better off this way. TT's been throwin' its weight around this country too damned long. It's time somebody put a stop to it!"

The dark one, Kiowa, murmured something again, his dark eyes watchfully probing.

Lou shouted angrily, "How the hell do I know how? I'll think of a way, don't you worry. And if that damned Johnny Toothaker even looks at me cross-eyed, I'll kill him!"

Dunn walked across to the table where the three sat. He was surprised at himself. He didn't like either Whitey or Kiowa, and he didn't like soreheads like Lou. Nor could he condone what Lou had done. But he heard himself saying, "Johnny just refused to sell me hay."

Lou shouted, "You see? This is the beginning. That Johnny Toothaker wants the whole country. Hell, I worked for 'em, didn't I? I know what their plans are. They got most of the graze in the country and most of the hayland, but it ain't enough. It never will be. Not until they own everything from Cottonwood Pass to the San Paulo range."

Nate stared down at him, a feeling of sympathy for and comradeship with Lou coming over him. Both of them had been hurt by Johnny Toothaker. It created a kind of bond.

And others were gathering curiously, having heard the exchange. Frank Dulane, from below Nate's place. Dewey Roark, two ranches below Dulane. Hank Stoner, from up on the left fork of Cottonwood Creek. Stoner queried, "What's this about Johnny refusing you hay?"

"He just did. Them stacks down by my fence that I always buy. He told me to hell with me, that TT needed all the hay they had this year."

Kiowa murmured, "They're just finished with playing it cute, that's all. Looks like you could see that. Johnny's a pusher, but up until now Sam Tolle's held him down. Sam makes out like TT's a great big good-hearted friend to everyone in the country. Took Lou's riling Johnny to make him show himself for what he really is."

Stoner murmured, his eyes a little scared, "Hell, I *got* to have TT hay this winter. I can't get through without it."

"Neither can I."

"But what the hell we goin' to do? They don't *have* to sell that hay."

Dulane was a powerful man in his mid-thirties, dark-faced and easily angered. He said, "I know what *I'm* goin' to do." His eyes were glittering, his mouth a thin, hard line. "I'm goin' to see Johnny Toothaker right now. *I'll* get this straightened out or know the reason why."

He looked around angrily, challengingly. "Who's comin' with me? Or are you goin' to let me go it alone?"

Kiowa said softly, "Maybe they'd rather beg.

Maybe they've got so used to lickin' TT's boots they can't do nothin' else."

He could have said nothing more carefully calculated to arouse the latent pride in the ranchers. It graveled them all to be dependent on TT bounty. Few men can take continuing favors without growing to resent the giver.

Not one of them, least of all Nate Dunn, stopped now to try and understand Johnny Toothaker. None tried to put himself into Johnny's boots. They didn't even consider that Johnny, hurt, jealous and humiliated, might have said something he didn't really mean; that he'd relent when he'd had a chance to calm down.

Dulane said harshly, "I'm goin'. If any of you are finished lickin' TT boots, you can come with me."

Nate said strongly, thinking of Will, thinking that Will would leave home if the cattle had to be sold, "I'll go, by God."

Stoner said, "Me too. Come on."

Roark hitched at his gun belt. Whitey got up from the table. He grinned down at Kiowa. "Keep Lou here. We'll be right back."

Following a now swaggering Dulane, the four marched out of the saloon.

Chapter Five

For a long time after Nate Dunn left, Johnny Toothaker stood at the bar, staring at the empty glass before him. There was faint nausea in his stomach now, and his head ached. He didn't want any more to drink.

Still, the irritation lingered with him, the smoldering anger. But coupled with it now was shame. Nate Dunn hadn't deserved what he'd given him. Nate Dunn hadn't done anything but ask about hay, hay that he'd always bought before, that he had a right to expect this year.

He glanced up at Lewt, the bartender. "See where Nate went?"

Lewt shook his head. "Out. After that I don't know. Way you roughed him up, he probably headed straight for the Boar's Head."

There was disapproval, cold and uncompromising in Lewt's eyes. It stirred anger in Johnny, but he fought it down. He said, "I'm sorry about that. I wanted to tell Nate."

"Try the Boar's Head," was all that Lewt would say. With a final, cold glance at Johnny, he turned away.

Johnny hesitated only a moment. He wasn't used to apologizing. He wasn't used to doing things that had to be apologized for. Then he turned and headed for the door.

A group of men, among them Nate Dunn, crowded in before he reached it. Their faces were flushed and angry, and the doors slammed in hard against the wall as they entered.

There was Nate Dunn, and Dulane, and Roark from below TT's boundaries. There was Stoner from up on the left fork of Cottonwood Creek. And there was Whitey Post, whom the whole country suspected of being an outlaw, from over at the foot of the San Paulo range.

They stopped inside the door. Their eyes were cold, their mouths thin lines in their angry faces. Johnny said, "Like to see you a minute, Nate."

Whitey grinned nastily and mimicked, "Like to see you a minute, Nate."

Johnny flushed. He put his eyes on Nate challengingly. Nate took a half step toward him, then halted uncertainly. He looked from one to another of his friends. He stopped, and a stubborn cast came to his jaw. He said, "What about?"

Johnny's temper was becoming increasingly hard to control. But he'd been in the wrong, and knew it, and consequently made a sterner effort. He said softly, "About the hay, Nate. I'm —"

"Sure he is!" scoffed Whitey contemptuously, anticipating Johnny's words. "Damn right he's sorry — now. Thing is, he ain't got the guts, to get nasty when there's a bunch of us."

Johnny stared at Whitey. "When did you buy chips in this?"

"Few minutes ago. I don't like to see people get pushed around."

Johnny took a step toward him, putting his weight down unexpectedly on his injured leg. Pain shot from the wound like a knife. And suddenly he remembered Lou's face, saw again that scene up at TT, Robin fleeing from the bunkhouse, Lou in pursuit.

Whitey pushed, while Johnny wavered. "Whole trouble with him is he's got a fast little piece for a wife and can't watch her and do his work too. So he's takin' it out on us."

It was an instant before Johnny's stunned mind comprehended this sudden switch in the conversation, before his startled ears could believe what they heard.

When they did, his anger of a few minutes before seemed like a puny thing. Thunderous, uncontrollable fury possessed his mind, until the faces before him blurred, until the blood drained out of his face and left it gray.

He didn't even think of his gun. All he thought was destroy, break, maim and kill. All he thought was that the mouth which had uttered those words had to be closed and smashed, and he lunged forward, the pain in his thigh forgotten now.

Whitey's eyes were briefly scared, and switched like lightning to the faces of the men beside him. His hand shot toward his gun, his expression now saying he knew he had gone too far.

Then Johnny's hard, bony fist exploded squarely in the middle of his mouth.

Whitey Post was flung back, as though by the kick of an outlaw horse. He struck the saloon wall with his shoulders and the impact rattled the glasses behind the bar on the other side of the room.

Not a knockout blow. But one which broke half a dozen of Whitey's teeth and smashed his lips against the broken stumps.

Stunned, he dragged the gun clear. Johnny, standing immediately over him, kicked out and it skittered noisily across the floor.

Johnny stooped to yank Whitey to his feet, the others forgotten, everything forgotten save for this burning need to destroy.

Nate Dunn struck him from behind, a sledging blow that nearly broke his neck. Johnny pitched forward, collapsing on top of the struggling Whitey Post.

For an instant, it was a tangle of flying arms and legs, as both men tried to gain their feet.

Johnny made it first, and climbed up the wall until he stood, head hanging, eyes dull and sick, with his back against it.

The fever was in them now, in them all. Blood had been drawn, and there was the unspoken obligation in their minds to Whitey Post for having taken their parts.

None stopped to consider Whitey's motives in doing so. None stopped to realize that Whitey was not an idealistic person given to taking the part of the underdog.

A kind of madness was on them, compounded of the resentment of years at having had to accept favors from Johnny Toothaker and Sam Tolle, and guilt because they resented when they ought to be grateful.

Nate Dunn circled to the right; Dulane waded in from the front, and Stoner came from the left. Roark, the most level-headed of the four, stared down at Whitey Post, his eyes questioning and a little puzzled as though he were wondering just why Whitey had stirred this up with his unnecessarily nasty remark about Johnny's wife. So far as Roark knew, she was a good woman. She wasn't the first that one of the hands had made a try for and she wouldn't be the last. The important thing in Roark's mind was that she *had* tried to get away.

Dulane's fist struck Johnny high on the forehead, snapped his head back against the wall with a thud. Stoner, a scrawny, red-haired man, swung for Johnny's belly and doubled him up. Dunn, not to be left out, snapped Johnny's head back again with a third blow that landed squarely on his right eye.

And now, Johnny, as though fighting for his life, came away from the wall, arms windmilling, fists striking without direction and without much force. He was virtually out on his feet from the quick combination of blows he had received. He was fighting half conscious, but there was an indomitable spirit about the way he did that made Roark yell, "Let up! That's enough!"

Johnny went down and they piled on top of him. Dulane seized a chair leg that had been broken off by Johnny's fall and began to beat him over the head with it.

Roark opened his mouth to yell again just as the doors slammed back and Sam Tolle burst into the saloon.

Sam took in the situation with a single, lightning glance. His hand snaked out his gun and he fired three quick shots over the heads of the bunch fighting on the floor. He roared, "Break it up! Or I'll by God break some heads!"

Dunn and Stoner looked up, startled, and stared at Sam stupidly. Dulane kept belaboring Johnny over the head with the chairleg, which, though inflicting painful bruises and cuts, was doing no serious damage.

Sam's face darkened. He took three quick strides to Dulane, and brought the gun barrel down in a savage, slashing motion.

Its sound, striking Dulane's skull, was dull and sodden. Dulane pitched sideways, unconscious before he struck the floor.

Sam put a boot in the middle of Dunn's chest and pushed. Dunn toppled back from his kneeling position and sprawled on the floor. Stoner scrambled like a startled badger to get out of the way.

Sam Tolle glared at Lewt, the bartender. "You son-of-a-bitch! Get me a pan of water, a towel, and a bottle of whisky. Then get the doc."

"He had it comin', damn —"

Sam's voice was deadly. "You open your mouth again and I'll close it for you! If it wasn't for Johnny and me you'd have gone broke five years ago. Now move!"

Johnny heard all this vaguely, as though from a distance. He heard footsteps coming toward him, felt Sam kneeling beside him to roll him onto his back.

Sam growled softly, "The dirty bastards!"

Johnny tried to grin. His lips were smashed and thick, his head light. He mumbled, "My fault."

"Your fault hell! You couldn't have done anything bad enough to make five of them jump you. I know you better than that!"

Johnny tried to argue, but he hadn't the strength. Sam lifted his head and poured a little whisky into his mouth. It burned like hell as it hit the cuts on his lips and inside his mouth, but going down it was warm and seemed to revive him a little.

He had a vague impression of men walking over him, and realized that Dunn and the others were shuffling past on their way out. Sam didn't even look at them. He dampened the towel in the pan Lewt had brought and dabbed at the cuts and bruises on Johnny's face as gently as a woman might have done.

Between the cold water, the whisky, and his own stamina, he began to regain full consciousness. He struggled to sit up, wincing as he did. Sam helped him.

The saloon was empty now, save for Dulane, unconscious, a few feet away. Johnny said, "Did I knock *him* out?"

"Huh uh. I did. The bastard was beatin' you with a chair leg and wouldn't stop."

Johnny grinned ruefully. "Guess I didn't do much good. I'm glad of that."

"You hurt Whitey bad enough. He was still spittin' teeth when he staggered out the door."

Johnny didn't answer, and after a moment Sam asked, "What the hell was it all about?"

Johnny stared at a button on the front of Sam's shirt. He licked his lips. "Me. I started it. Dunn came over to ask about hay and I told him he didn't get it this year."

"Why'n hell did you do that? You knew we intended to let him have them stacks down by his fence."

Johnny shrugged and shook his head. "I don't know." His eyes lifted and met Sam's determinedly. "Yes I do know too. Dunn said he'd been up at the house while we were gone. I —"

Sam began to grin. "You didn't think Robin would look at that old bastard, did you?"

"I suppose not. Not really." He hesitated

a moment. "Ever been jealous, Sam? It's a dirty, lousy feeling. It makes you want to —"

Sam interrupted. "You got nothing to be jealous about. Sore, yes. Sore at Lou. But you paid him off for bothering Robin. Broke his arm and fired him. Let it drop there. You don't have to pay off anybody else. You sure as hell don't have to get even with Robin. Worst thing she did was get lonesome, and go out to talk to Lou."

Doc Peabody came storming grumpily in, carrying his scuffed black bag. Behind him came Lewt Rhea. Lewt stared at Sam Tolle uncertainly.

Johnny knew Sam wouldn't have blamed Lewt if the fight had been anywhere near even. Now he figured Sam would order the TT hands to stay the hell away from the Stag.

He said, "I got what was coming to me, Sam. Let it go at that."

Most of the irritation and bad temper was gone from Johnny. He could think of Robin now without getting mad. In fact, thinking of her now he was feeling shame, and an overpowering desire to hold her and make things right with her again.

Funny, he thought, what a chain of events could be set in motion by an apparently insignificant thing. Robin had been lonesome because Johnny had been gone so long. Wanting someone to talk to, she'd gone to hunt Lou up. And Lou had reached a wrong conclusion.

Everything had gone on from there. Lou had a broken arm; Johnny was partially crippled from a pitchfork wound. Whitey Post had six tooth stumps in the front of his mouth, the pain of which was probably driving him almost crazy. Sam was sore at Lewt Rhea and at Dulane, Dunn, Stoner and Roark. And they were sore at TT.

Doc was putting iodine on Johnny's face cuts and then strips of court plaster. Every time he touched the iodine swab to his face, Johnny winced with pain. And every time he winced, Doc grunted with satisfaction.

Johnny grinned. "You old bastard, you like to hurt people, don't you?"

"Not people. Just you. Of all the nasty —"

Johnny said, "I'm sorry, Doc," and meant it.

Doc peered into his face. He mumbled something to himself, without smiling, without changing expression, but when he resumed treating Johnny's face, his hands were gentler, his eyes more filled with compassion.

He finished, and began to stow his things in his bag. Sam said, "Whitey Post probably wants you next. He's over at the Boar's Head,

I reckon, with a mouthful of broken teeth."

Doc looked at Johnny irritably. "You all through for tonight? I'd like to get some sleep. I was up the whole damned night with that Hostedder woman up on the Blue."

Johnny said, "I'm all through. You take care of Whitey and then you can go to bed."

Doc said sarcastically, "That's good of you. Thanks." He picked up his bag and went out into the street.

Johnny got stiffly to his feet. He limped to the door.

It was over. Or so it seemed. But a little core of worry was beginning to stir in Johnny's mind. Lou Saks, carrying a grudge, could be dangerous. So could Whitey Post. Then he put the thought away. They'd have to handle whatever happened. They always had.

He said, "Come on, Sam. Let's go home."

Chapter Six

The pain of Johnny's blow, the one which broke his teeth, was not immediately felt by Whitey Post. His mouth felt numb, and his shoulders struck the wall, knocking part of the wind out of him. He slid down the wall to the floor, grabbing for his gun.

Johnny kicked it away, nearly breaking his hand in the process. Then Johnny yanked him to his feet.

Then something else happened. The others ganged up on Johnny, and Whitey slid back to the floor.

He looked stupidly around for his gun, saw it halfway across the room and began to crawl toward it.

He was only half conscious but he didn't realize it. He kept wondering why he was crawling instead of walking upright. Then, as he sucked a big breath of air in through his open mouth, he felt the pain of it passing across the raw nerve ends of his broken teeth.

It was blinding, maddening. He closed his mouth and sucked at the tooth stumps, his face twisted almost unrecognizably with the excruciating pain. He put a hand over his mouth, as though this could further warm the teeth, chilled by that breath of air.

Gradually, the pain subsided. By the time Whitey again became aware of what was going on, Johnny Toothaker was down and Dulane was beating him over the head with a chair leg.

Then Sam came in. After that, Whitey didn't want any more fight. He only wanted to get away. So while Sam Tolle was occupied with the others, he got painfully to his feet and slunk out the doors into the street, keeping his mouth carefully closed and breathing through his nose.

He stumbled across the street to the Boar's Head. He went in, scowling at the curious glances he got, and went directly to the bar.

Kiowa left Lou and came straight to him, carrying a bottle and glass. He set the glass down carefully on the bar and poured it about half full. His eyes were still, watchful, and if he was curious at this unexpected turn of affairs he didn't show it. He said expression-lessly, "What happened?"

Whitey glared at him and spit blood at his feet. He snatched up the glass and gulped it down. Then he bent double, holding his mouth with both hands and whimpering softly like a hurt dog.

It was a long time before he straightened. When he did, he stubbornly poured the glass full and gulped it again. Again he bent double, holding his mouth, shaking, making small noises. But this spell didn't last so long. He straightened sooner.

He looked Kiowa straight in the eye and mumbled thickly over his puffy lips and broken teeth, "The dirty, stinkin', son-of-a-bitch! I'll kill him. I'll kill him if it's the last damn thing I ever do!"

Kiowa didn't comment. Neither did he show emotion. He said, "Better see Doc first. Get those damn stumps yanked out."

"You go to hell! I want 'em in my mouth just like they are. I want the goddamn things to hurt. So I'll remember who did this to me. So I'll keep on wantin' to kill him more than anything else in the world."

Kiowa shrugged almost imperceptibly. His eyes glittered briefly, perhaps from satisfaction, perhaps from some other emotion.

The liquor was beginning to make itself felt now. It warmed Whitey's belly, soared dizzyingly to his head. He looked at the glass, weighed his need against the pain of drinking.

With sudden determination, he poured the glass half full for a third time. He gulped it, taking care that he didn't pour it directly on the stumps of his broken teeth. He gagged a little, but this time pain didn't bend him double. It only twisted his face.

He could feel the liquor beginning to take hold. But the virulence of his anger didn't fade. He could still think of nothing but killing Johnny Toothaker, and the only effect of the liquor on this compulsion was that it deluded his mind into thinking that killing Johnny might not only be possible, it might be relatively easy.

Kiowa and Whitey Post had long had their eyes on TT cattle. They'd planned the theft of TT's beef herd for three years running, but they'd never gone through with it even though Kiowa knew an Indian Agent over in Utah that would take the lot, no questions asked. Stealing from TT was just too damned dangerous — as long as Johnny Toothaker and Sam Tolle were alive and well. But if they weren't —

Right now Lou Saks was itching for a chance

to kill Johnny. And so was Whitey Post.

Lou's trouble with Johnny had been unplanned. The developments which followed had been extremely lucky. But now it was up to Whitey and Kiowa to pick it up and carry it from here. With help from an unsuspecting Lou, from TT's unsuspecting neighbors.

Whitey stared at Lou, now approaching from the table. He spoke softly to Kiowa. "I want Johnny Toothaker myself. Let Lou have Sam Tolle."

For the first time Kiowa's face showed expression. He said impatiently, "Don't be stupid. Lou gets them both. Then, while the law and the TT crew is busy chasing Lou, we take the cattle."

"But —"

Disgust was heavy in Kiowa's voice. "Just because your goddam teeth hurt you is no reason to ball up the whole deal. We might not get another chance like this one as long as we live. Go get your stupid teeth pulled. Then maybe you'll be able to think straight again."

Lou came up beside them and Kiowa's mouth clamped shut. Lou had an injured air, as though he were put out at having been left sitting alone at the table when all this was of vital concern to him. He asked, "What the hell happened, anyway? You mean Johnny whipped the five of you?"

Kiowa gave him a bleak smile. "He sure as hell did. Or damned near to it. Next time —"

Lou said, "Next time let me take care of that son-of-a-bitch. I'll get the job done right."

Kiowa appeared to consider Lou's proposal. As angry as he was, as maddened by pain, Whitey couldn't help feeling a stir of admiration. Kiowa had managed it, with no apparent effort, so that Lou was begging to be sent after Johnny.

At last Kiowa said thoughtfully, "I don't think so. If somebody kills Johnny, somebody else would have to kill Sam Tolle. With either one of them around, we don't dare make a move."

Lou's eyes brightened. "What kind of move? What are you talking about?" There was a dawning suspicion in his eyes.

Kiowa glanced questioningly at Whitey. "What do you think? Should we tell him?"

Whitey shook his head, knowing this was expected of him.

Lou's face darkened. "Damn it, what's going on? This is my business too, you know. Johnny and Sam Tolle gave me forty-eight hours to get out of the country."

Kiowa appeared to reach a decision. "All

right. I'll tell you. But if I do, you're in it same as we are. Understand?"

Lou nodded doubtfully.

"We've had our eyes on the TT beef herd every fall for three years only we've been afraid to try for it on account of Johnny and Sam. This year — what with the trouble you stirred up, and the trouble between Johnny and his neighbors that Whitey just stirred up — well, we might be able to pull it off."

Lou's eyes gleamed greedily. "What do I get out of it?"

Kiowa stared at him coldly, until Lou's eyes dropped. "A share. How much depends on how much you do."

"What 'if I get rid of both Johnny and Sam?"

"You won't. You haven't got that much guts."

Lou's face grew angry instantly, and Kiowa said swiftly, placatingly, "Besides, that ain't the smart way to handle it. Why should any of us stick our necks out? Let Johnny's neighbors do the job. Hell, you know 'em, Lou. They trust you an' they're leery of us. You work on 'em. Then, when the time comes, if you still want to, you can lead 'em and maybe take care of Johnny and Sam at the same time. After that's done, I reckon you'd like to finish what you started this afternoon with Johnny's wife." He grinned suggestively and when Kiowa grinned, which he seldom did, it was the kind of grin that made you want to shudder.

A gleam came into Lou Saks' eyes as he thought of that.

Kiowa said, "All right then. Get out and find 'em. They're sore now, plenty sore. See that you keep 'em that way."

Lou stared at him for a moment, obviously debating whether or not he wanted to take orders from him. He must have thought about a share of the TT herd in those seconds. Then he nodded, and walking in an oddly awkward way to protect his broken arm, he went out through the doors to the street.

Doc Peabody came stomping through the doors, carrying his scuffed bag. He came to the bar and set the bag on it. He opened it and took out a pair of wicked-looking, nickel-plated tooth pulling forceps. He said, "Johnny sent me to take care of those broken teeth. You want 'em pulled standin' up, or are you goin' to sit down?" He stared at Whitey irritably, with ill-concealed dislike. Then he grumbled, "TT's footing the bill, if that's what's worrying you."

"It ain't. Just take your damn horseshoe

nippers an' get the hell out of here."

Doc scowled and began to replace the forceps. Kiowa murmured placatingly, "Wait a minute, Doc. He ain't thinkin' straight. Go on over there to that table and get ready. I'll talk to him."

Doc went over to the table and laid both bag and forceps on it. Kiowa stared at Whitey. No expression showed in his face, but looking into his eyes was like looking into a particularly dark corner of hell. Whitey felt a small chill touch his spine. Damn it, he shouldn't ever have taken up with this one. He couldn't understand the man, and sometimes he wasn't even sure Kiowa was a man. He could feign a kind of warmth and kid around with other men, but he was always withdrawn inside, always off in some dark place by himself.

And he got what he wanted from Whitey every time just by looking at him in this strange, cold way.

Whitey sucked a breath in through his mouth. Pain shot like knives from the broken stumps. He said angrily, "All right, damn you! All right! I'll let Doc pull 'em if it's that —"

Kiowa's face mirrored brief satisfaction. "Good. Get on over there and sit down. There's over a thousand steers in that TT beef herd and Kincheloe will pay us thirty dollars a head for 'em. Think about that while Doc's pulling your teeth. Because it'll take some straight thinking before we get 'em to Kincheloe."

Whitey went over to the table and sat down. Kiowa came up behind him and seized his head between two wiry, incredibly strong hands. Doc got a good grip on the forceps and when Whitey fearfully opened his mouth, he went to work.

Pain, continuous and nearly unbearable, began. Every time Doc put those damned cold forceps on a tooth, pain seemed to shoot clear to Whitey's groin.

Only one thing helped him and kept him conscious. Hatred. Hatred and a promise of revenge that he made to himself repeatedly as Doc worked.

At last the job was done, and Doc wiped his bloody hands on a towel brought to him for that purpose by the bartender. He repacked his bag, muttered something at Whitey, and stomped outside.

And now, Whitey realized something he had not realized before. Tonight he had aged by fifteen years. He was like an old gummer cow, like an old man. His mouth had come together and shrunk up and would stay that way unless Whitey was willing to have the others pulled and get himself a set of white, clacking store teeth.

He looked at Kiowa with sullen defiance. He spoke thickly, as though with a mouthful of food. "You do whatever you goddam please about the cattle. But Johnny's mine. And if you don't like that, you can damn well go to hell."

Kiowa shrugged fatalistically. But he didn't reply.

Lou Saks, after leaving the Boar's Head, crossed the street at a careful, shuffling walk to the Stag. Johnny Toothaker and Sam Tolle were gone. But the others were there, Dulane, Dunn, Stoner and Roark.

They were clustered together at one end of the bar, their faces worried, talking in low tones. They all looked a little flabbergasted, as though wondering how all this had happened, what it had stemmed from, and why it had blown up so disastrously and suddenly tonight.

Lou saw something else in all of them. Fear. Desperation. All of them, in attacking Johnny Toothaker had taken an ill-considered, disastrous step. They had incurred the anger of TT and they couldn't afford to. Nor did they know how they could get back into TT's good graces, or even if they could.

For the briefest moment, Lou weakened in his hatred of Johnny and of TT. He had started all this earlier in the evening himself. He had made a try for Johnny's wife and from that simple thing had snowballed all this trouble, for himself, for the four at the bar, for Whitey Post.

He forgot the broken arm for an instant and tried to raise it to fumble automatically for papers and tobacco. The tightening of the muscles brought an agonizing wave of pain.

And his regret died as quickly as it had been born. Johnny hadn't had to be so damn rough. It wasn't *all* Lou's fault. That woman of Johnny's had been partly to blame. She hadn't been asked to come to the bunkhouse. She'd come of her own free will.

He stepped toward the four at the bar. He didn't feel good, but he knew this had to be done tonight. Show them a way out of the trouble they were in — at least make them think it was a way out — before they went home and talked things over with their wives. At least keep their resentment burning high.

Lou forced himself to grin in a friendly way at them. It was a twisted, painful grin, and forced, but they didn't seem to notice. They welcomed him as one of them, one who had also suffered at the hands of TT. And Lou stepped into their tight little group.

Chapter Seven

As they stepped out into the street, Sam Tolle looked at Johnny. "How's the leg? Want me to hire a rig?"

Johnny shook his head, subdued and quiet. He had more hurts than the leg now and ached all over every time he moved. But he was also troubled by a deep sense of shame. His jealousy had stirred up a frightening amount of trouble tonight, and he was convinced now that it had been unfounded, that it had been based on his own sense of insecurity.

Tomorrow, he'd ride down to Dunn's place and reassure the man that hay would be available just as it always had. He'd see Roark and Stoner and Dulane as well. He'd let them know that tonight's happenings were going to be forgotten. It wouldn't be easy to see those four, to approach them with humility after the way they'd beaten him tonight, but easy or not, it was something he had to do. Otherwise, ill feeling and resentment would fester like a sore, and spread. Johnny had seen these things before, and knew how they could sweep a country.

He untied his horse, swung stiffly and painfully to the saddle. As he reined out into the street, Sam Tolle came up beside him. Together they rode out of town at a slow trot.

Sam didn't talk. Neither did Johnny, for several miles. At last Johnny pulled his thoughts from Robin long enough to say, "I'll ride down and see Dunn and Dulane and Stoner and Roark tomorrow. I started this and it's up to me to set it right."

"All right Johnny. But if you don't feel up to it, I'll be glad to do it for you."

Johnny chuckled mirthlessly. "I won't feel up to it, but I've got to do it anyhow."

They rode on, then, in silence for several miles. At last Johnny could hold the question that was troubling him no longer. "How about Robin, Sam? What am I going to say to her?"

For a moment, Sam didn't reply. At last he said, "Distrust ain't an easy thing to forgive, Johnny. But I got an idea Robin will make the grade. Just tell her what you feel. Just tell her you're sorry."

"I am sorry, Sam. I feel like a sonofabitch."

"You acted like one too." There was a smile in Sam's voice. "But for a guy with a pitchfork wound in his leg, you done all right. They'll want more'n five before they try tacklin' you again."

Johnny thought of Lou Saks. In spite of himself, anger stirred in him. He fought it down determinedly. He didn't know what he was going to do about Lou. He'd laid down an ultimatum — leave the country within forty-eight hours. And he'd have to follow through on it or lose the respect of the whole country, a thing he couldn't afford the way things were.

Well, he'd think about that tomorrow. Right now the main thing was to make his peace with Robin.

His nervousness increased as they neared the ranch. It was late. Suppose she'd gone to bed? Suppose she was asleep? Then he'd have to wait until morning because he didn't want to waken her. He didn't want to risk trying to make his peace with her until everything was right for it. It would be touchy enough anyway.

A new thought struck him, one that put terror into his heart. What if she refused to accept his apologies? What if she was already preparing to leave him? Or had already left?

He realized that he couldn't blame her if she had. But he unconsciously began to hurry his horse in spite of the added pain of doing so.

He brought the ranchhouse into sight as he and Sam came around a bend in the road, and for an instant relief touched him. The house was ablaze with light.

Then the relief was gone. A house ablaze with light at this hour was more ominous than reassuring.

They rode down the lane into the yard, and Johnny dismounted stiffly. He handed up the reins to Sam. "Wish me luck, Sam."

"I do. Go on now."

Johnny walked toward the house. He'd faced many things in his time, none so hard as this. But he'd faced them without turning tail and he'd do the same now. He limped to the porch and clumped up the two steps to it. He opened the door and went inside.

Robin stood on the far side of the room, staring into the huge fireplace where there was a fire crackling against the night's chill. The flickering light from the flames highlighted her face and the hollows of her cheeks and throat. She turned her head and looked at Johnny like a little girl, her eyes enormous, her mouth full and uncertain.

He limped toward her. "Robin —"

She came running toward him, tears welling from her eyes, her fine chin quivering. Johnny caught her and held her hard against him for a long, long, wonderful moment.

It had not been hard — because Robin was the way she was. But he didn't want it forgotten, unspoken between them. He said, his face against her fragrant hair, "I'm sorry. I've never been more sorry for anything in my life."

"Don't talk about it, Johnny. It's over."

Over. Between the two of them it was. But not finished so far as the rest of the country was concerned. Lou Saks was packing a murderous hate. So was Whitey Post. So were the four TT's neighbors, who had attacked Johnny in the Stag tonight.

Johnny's arms tightened. He said, "How big a damn fool can a man be?"

She smiled up at him shakily. "I'm not very old, Johnny, and I'm not a very good wife. But I'll try to learn."

He snorted.

"I mean it, Johnny. I shouldn't even have gone near that bunkhouse. I just got lonely." Her eyes did not quite meet his and he got the sudden feeling that there was more to it than this. Else she would not have been so willing to make up and forget.

Jealousy touched him again, but this time he surprised himself with his tolerance. He remembered a woman he'd known years before, remembered being attracted to her and feeling she was attracted to him even though she was his neighbor's wife.

Nothing had come of it, and neither Johnny nor the woman had wanted it to. Nor had it affected her marriage.

Such things happened to people, he guessed. Becoming insanely jealous only gave them more importance than they deserved.

He released her and sank to a couch covered with cowhide. She sat beside him, her face gentle with concern. "Are you hurt badly? Is there anything I can do?"

He grinned, feeling good again for the first time since he'd ridden in this afternoon. "I'm all right. Just sit there and let me look at you."

"I'll get you something to eat. And some coffee."

He nodded and watched her hurry away toward the kitchen. He wanted her suddenly, wanted her close against him, warm and soft and eager. He felt his blood pound harder through his veins.

He got up and followed her into the kitchen. He sat down straddling a chair and watched her work.

This was the commonplace, the familiar. She was deft with her hands, and moved with the grace of a girl, humming softly to herself as she did. Occasionally she would look at him and when she did, her eyes would smile and warm for him.

Johnny sighed with satisfaction. Today had brought trouble, but all was right again between himself and Robin. That was what mattered. And he'd work hard at making things stay this way. No more senseless jealousy. A part of love was trust.

And yet, a nagging worry hung unspoken in the back of his mind. The trouble which had come today was not yet gone.

He tried to understand how it had flared so suddenly in town tonight. It couldn't have flared like that out of no more than his refusal to sell hay to Dunn unless resentment and hate were already there, brooding, sleeping, in the backs of his neighbors' minds.

And that pair from over at the foot of the San Paulos — Whitey Post and the one called Kiowa — they'd added fuel to the flames of hatred by instigating and leading the attack on him.

Robin saw his worried look and asked, "What's the matter?"

Johnny shrugged, wishing he could shrug off the worry itself. "It's something that happened in town. The fight."

"What started the fight, Johnny?"

He stared at her, a rueful smile touching the corners of his mouth. "Me, I guess. I was sore-headed as a snake being prodded with a stick. I — well, Dunn came up and made one of those sly remarks he's always making. Only it didn't seem funny tonight. I blew up and refused to sell him hay. He went across the street and apparently got everybody else worked up. That pair from over at the foot of the San Paulo mountains didn't help any either."

"What pair?"

"One of 'em's just called Kiowa. The other's Whitey Post."

She turned quickly back to the stove. She was busy for several moments, turning the strips of bacon she was cooking for him. When she turned back to face him, her expression was composed. Yet he couldn't rid himself of the impression that one of those names, either that of Kiowa or Whitey, had upset her.

She said firmly, "You and Sam have been good to those men. You've let them run their cattle with yours in the summer. You've given them winter range, and you've sold them hay at a fair price. I don't see what they've got to be worked up about."

Johnny grinned. "Ranchers are a funny breed. They're so damned independent it hurts. They don't like us for helping them. They resent us because they're forced by necessity to accept our help."

The door opened, and Sam came in. He glanced from one to the other searchingly, saw what he had hoped to see and grinned as widely and happily as a boy on his birthday. "I see it's all patched up," he said.

Johnny said, "If I ever pull anything like I did this evening again, Sam, — well, you boot me good."

"Don't worry. I will."

Robin's face was still worried. "I feel responsible for all this. How is it going to come out, Sam? Will it be all right?"

"You mean Dunn and the others? Sure it'll be all right. They'll smolder for a while, but they'll get over it. Johnny's going down first thing in the morning and see them. Once they know they're going to get the hay they need they'll be all right."

"I hope so," she said fervently. "I surely hope so."

She brought him a plate of bacon strips, fried eggs and fried potatoes and set it in front of him. Coffee was simmering on the back of the stove, and she poured him a mugful, then sat down across the table from him.

Johnny ate hungrily, surprised at his appetite, even though he'd had no supper. He sipped the scalding coffee gratefully.

Robin watched him, and if he had glanced up and seen the expression in her eyes as she did, there would have been no further doubt in his mind, now or ever again, as to whether or not she truly loved him.

Sam got up. "I'll take a turn around the yard. Then I'm going to bed. I suggest you two do the same."

Johnny finished his coffee and glanced up. He felt warm, and alive, and good. He watched Sam open the door and step outside.

Robin started to say something, but stopped as the door flung open and banged against the wall.

Sam Tolle stood in the doorway again, his face dark with fury. His eyes gleamed dangerously and his mouth was a thin, straight line. He said, "Get out here Johnny! Get out here and see what those lousy bastards have done!"

Something cold lay close to Johnny's spine. He jumped to his feet, nearly falling as he put his weight on his injured leg.

Robin's face was white, her eyes scared. She followed him to the door, stepped out behind him and came up close at his side. He could feel her body trembling, and put an automatic, protective arm around her waist.

His eyes were rooted on something down the valley, something that showed up clearly in the utter darkness of night. Haystacks were burning down there, putting a dull, red glow in the sky.

He knew instantly and without thinking which haystacks they were. They were the ones which nestled close to Nathan Dunn's north fence.

Chapter Eight

Only for a moment did they stand there staring at the glow in the sky. Then Sam Tolle's great voice rolled across the yard, "Saddle up! Damn it, roll out and saddle up!"

He was running even as he shouted. Johnny pulled away from Robin and limped across the yard in his wake. Robin ran beside him. "Couldn't it have been an accident? Some boys smoking or something?"

Johnny didn't reply. His own mind had seized upon that possibility because he didn't want to think the stacks had been fired deliberately. But he knew it had been no accident.

The bunkhouse door burst open and the crew spilled out into the yard, some of them dressing as they came. Arleigh Peters growled, "Best damn hand I've held all night. And I had to throw it away!"

Johnny said, "Play it when you get back."

"Who'll believe—?" Johnny lost the rest as Peters ran past him.

Horses milled in the dark corral, rearing, whinnying, galloping around in a frightened group. Ropes hissed as they snaked out and one by one the men led their mounts through the gate to saddle them outside.

Johnny got his own rope off his saddle resting on the top pole of the corral. His leg was bothering him now, stiffening and very painful. He went into the corral, roped a horse and led him outside. The others were waiting impatiently for him.

He bridled the horse, then threw his saddle on and cinched it down. He looked at Robin, standing silent and scared, a shadow in the darkness. He said, "The rest of you go on. I'll catch up."

They thundered away in a group. One of them uttered a high, thin yell.

Dust swirled around Johnny, rolling past him and over Robin's still, waiting shape. Leading the horse, he walked to her.

He said calmly, "I'm all right now. And I'll be back soon."

"Your leg. You shouldn't—"

"I stirred this up. It's up to me to

set it straight."

"I did, you mean. It's my fault. Oh Johnny, I'm so sorry!"

He put his hands on her shoulders. He bent his head and kissed her on the mouth. His voice was gruff, but strong with feeling. "You've got nothing to be sorry for. Wait up for me."

He swung to his horse and thundered out of the yard. Robin stood in the swirling dust watching him until he disappeared into darkness. Then she turned and walked slowly toward the house.

Johnny reined through the wire gate, left open by the crew, and spurred recklessly across the hayfield. He rode straight toward the flaming stacks several miles away.

He could feel blood soaking the bandage on his leg as he rode. He could feel the beginning of an odd lightheadedness caused by loss of blood. But he knew bleeding would cleanse the wound, that it was probably good for him even if it made him weak.

He rode hard for nearly two miles before he saw the galloping shapes of Sam and the others ahead. When they hauled in beside the burning stacks, he was no more than fifty feet behind.

As Johnny had expected, there was no one here. But a hundred and fifty tons of hay in three big stacks was shooting flame and smoke two hundred feet into the black night sky.

Arleigh Peters said, "Rain might save 'em, boss, but nothin' else will."

Johnny and Sam stared at the stacks helplessly. It made a man furious to think that practically none of the hay had really been destroyed as yet. Only the outsides of the stacks. Inside, the hay was green and good, untouched by flame and smoke. They'd burn for a while like this, until the loose hay on the sides and top had been consumed. Then they'd smolder — maybe for weeks — until fire ate all the way to the ground.

Horses fidgeted uneasily in the leaping glare of the flames, held in place only by the iron hands of their riders. The men looked at Sam and Johnny — and waited.

At last Sam yelled, "Nate Dunn did this! He was sore because you refused him the hay. Figured if he couldn't have it, nobody else could either."

Johnny said, "Maybe." He was thinking that usually he was the hothead in this partnership — the doer. Sam was the patient one. Only tonight it seemed to be the other way around. Sam didn't have to put his feelings into words. Johnny knew what he wanted.

He didn't look at Sam and he didn't look at young Will Dunn, who had spent the summer riding with the TT crew.

Whatever they did tonight, or didn't do, Nate Dunn was finished on Cottonwood Creek. He'd never get another spear of hay from TT. Johnny saw that knowledge in young Will's face.

Arleigh Peters shouted over the roar of the burning stacks, "Let's go! Let's go see, by God, what Nate has got to say!"

Sam Tolle eased his plunging horse over beside that of Peters. There were two groups now — and young Will Dunn sitting his horse all alone between.

Johnny yelled, "Whether Nate did this or not, it's sure he's seen the fire. What's he going to think and what's he going to do when TT comes riding into his yard?"

"Hope the bastard does fight!" This came from someone in the group.

Johnny shouted, "He will. Nate may be a lot of things but he's not a coward. Before anybody rides down there, we'd all better make up our minds how far we're prepared to go. Maybe we'd better hold a trial right here and decide whether Nate's guilty of setting this fire or not. Because when we ride to his house, we're going to have action."

That calmed them down a little but not enough. Sam Tolle was scowling savagely, but

Johnny knew him like a book. Sam was realizing that Johnny's words were true. Nate Dunn, seeing TT ride into his yard in a body, having seen the burning stacks, would know he had been tried and convicted by TT of setting them afire. He'd meet them with rifle fire, maybe killing or wounding one or more of them before they got to him.

Sam growled, "Who else—?"

Johnny said, "Maybe somebody that wanted us to blame Nate. The whole town knows I refused Nate that hay. The whole town knows about the fight. Whitey and Kiowa stirred up the fight. Why not this too?"

He could feel Will Dunn's eyes on him. He glanced reassuringly at Will. The look in the boy's eyes embarrassed him.

Sam asked sourly, "What do *you* want to do?"

"Go on back home. Let the sheriff handle this."

Sam stared at him unbelievingly. "You don't sound much like the Johnny Toothaker I know."

Johnny grinned. "What am I supposed to do, breathe fire?"

Arleigh Peters said, "Johnny, if Nate gets away with this— Hell, everybody that's sore at us will figure we're getting soft."

Johnny opened his mouth to say that nobody

was sore at TT. Then he clamped it shut. The fight in town tonight had showed him otherwise. A lot of people carried grudges against TT. Not because of anything TT had done to them, either. Because of the things TT had done for them.

He stared uncompromisingly at Peters. "Nobody will make that mistake twice."

Peters shrugged. "I ain't bucking you, Johnny. You're the boss. You and Sam. You settle this between the two of you."

Johnny looked at Sam. "What about it, Sam?"

Sam shrugged. "Whatever you do is all right with me."

Johnny stared at the crew. "Then let's go home."

A long sigh of relief, inaudible to the others because of the fire's noise, but not to Johnny, escaped the tense lips of Will Dunn. The others turned their horses and headed home. Johnny followed, and Will fell in beside him.

The boy was nearly as tall as Johnny, but there was no body to him. He was wiry to the point of being skinny. His hair, yellow as straw and almost as coarse, stood out in a shock in front of his tipped-back hat. He had a thin fuzz of yellow whiskers on his smooth face, fuzz that had never yet felt the edge of a razor.

Freckles bridged his nose, not little ones but

big, brown ones and his face was always red, never tanning like those of the other men. He began, "Mr. Toothaker – Johnny–"

Johnny said, "I gave your dad a bad time tonight just because I was sore about something else. I guess he owed me this."

"He didn't – he couldn't of done it. It wouldn't make no sense."

"When a man gets soreheaded, Will, nothing makes much sense." He didn't share Will's belief that his father hadn't fired the stacks. He thought Nate had done it, sure as hell. But even if he had, he didn't deserve to die for it and that was what he'd have done if Johnny and Sam and the TT crew had ridden down there tonight.

Will said, "This'll mean we have to get rid of our stock."

"Maybe not. Maybe something can be worked out yet."

After that, he rode in silence, only half aware of the boy riding at his side. His leg pained him and his lightheadedness had not decreased. The bandage on his leg still felt wet and warm.

That fight in town, erupting so violently and unexpectedly, had both shocked and unnerved him. Until it had erupted, he had believed that TT had the goodwill of its neighbors. God knew they'd tried hard enough to earn it.

But he'd reckoned without the jealousy and resentment of poor, struggling men toward their rich and successful neighbors. He had reckoned without their pride, hurt every year at having to accept help from Toothaker and Tolle.

The glow in the sky faded as they left the burning haystacks behind. The lights of the home place flickered faintly up ahead.

An uneasy feeling kept tugging at Johnny's troubled mind. Trying to rid himself of it, he made an effort to believe that whatever had started tonight was over and done. But deep inside he knew that it was not. Like a man beginning to slide with an avalanche, he knew that its destruction and terror had only begun.

He called himself a fool. But his certainty did not diminish.

Robin watched Johnny ride away after the others, and stood motionless in the dust raised by his horse until the hoofbeats died. She headed for the house, then changed her mind and walked around the corral to a place from which she could look down the long valley of Cottonwood Creek toward the blazing stacks.

She couldn't actually see the flame. But she could see the glow it put upon the sky above it. And in this glow she could see the billowing clouds of smoke.

Robin, too, was in the grip of terror, of uneasiness and premonition. Kiowa. The name had rung a bell of terror in her mind, when Johnny mentioned it tonight.

It made her remember a night in Denver before she'd met Johnny or even heard of him. A night two years ago.

In the midst of ugly violence, she'd heard that name spoken by one of two men who seized her as she was walking home and dragged her into an alleyway. Kiowa. A shudder took her and shook her body violently.

It couldn't be the same one. It couldn't be. Kiowa was the name of an Indian tribe. Probably fifty men carried it around as a nickname. But something cold lay along her spine.

For a long time after the attack, she'd thought she was going mad. She'd hated the thought of marriage. And then Johnny had come along, gentle and calm and good. She'd sensed that violence lived in him, but he'd always been patient with her. And he had conquered her fears so succesfully that she'd been able to come to him as a normal wife.

Now her fears were back. Not all men were like Johnny. There were those like Kiowa and his companion, those like Lou Saks, lusting and cruel and violent. She wanted suddenly for Johnny to be here, for his strong arms to be holding her and driving away her fears: fears that this Kiowa he had mentioned was the same one who had participated in the attack on her in Denver. Fears that with Johnny gone, he might come here.

She glanced around her into the dark shadows. Her flesh suddenly crawled. She turned and ran heedlessly for the house.

She slammed inside and bolted the door behind. Then, in the warm lamplight, in the familiar surroundings, her fears began to subside. She was being a coward. She was Johnny's wife now and a coward was something she must never be.

Resolutely, she turned and unbolted the door. She stepped out onto the great, wide veranda of the house.

She looked up at the tall peaks to northward, shifted her glance to the irregular line of hills directly to the east.

She was alone no more. She was Johnny Toothaker's wife. She loved him and he loved her and she was safe.

He would be hungry when he returned, and tired. His wound would be hurting him and would need fresh bandages. A good wife would have all these things for him, and more, when he returned. She would let him know, tonight, that his love for her was returned a hundredfold.

She turned to re-enter the house, her glance lingering on the horizon to the east, on the pale clouds silhouetting the jagged skyline.

And then she froze. For she saw something there that sent a cold chill of fear traveling again along her spine.

One by one, a file of horsemen crossed the ridge, briefly silhouetted against that pale patch of clouds as they did.

She counted twelve.

No ranch all along the Cottonwood, save for TT, employed twelve men. And TT's men were down below at those burning stacks.

Like ghosts, the distant riders disappeared from sight. They were gone, so completely gone that for an instant Robin wondered if she had not imagined them, if they were not specters dredged up by her own fearful mind.

But she knew that they were not. And she knew something else as well. They were up there for the purpose of hurting Johnny, and Sam, and TT Ranch.

Chapter Nine

Halfway back to the homeplace, Will Dunn let his horse fall behind, watching Johnny Tooth-aker closely as he did. But Johnny was too pre-occupied even to notice his absence, and went on ahead until he disappeared from sight into the darkness.

Will sat his horse for a long, long time, neither urging him on ahead nor turning back.

He felt very much alone with the tall peaks around him, with the shroud of darkness lying over the land. He could hear the faint burbling of the Cottonwood as it trickled lazily along down in the bottom. He could hear the stirring of field mice in the hayfield. He could hear the whirring, beating wings of an owl as it sped past overhead, hunting.

And he felt as though he were being hunted

himself. He felt helpless and confused and found that he was wholly unable to make the decision he knew he had to make.

Will Dunn was shocked that his father had fired those three haystacks: he did not doubt for a minute that his father was the one who had done it. He knew his father's pride — not as strong or stubborn as his grandfather's had been, perhaps, but strong enough. He knew that his father carried a deep resentment of Toothaker and Tolle because he was forced to depend upon them.

But he could sympathize with Johnny too. Johnny had been hurt and out of sorts when he talked to Nate Dunn in town. He could hardly be blamed for losing his temper and saying something he didn't mean.

If Will's father had gone on home, if he'd been willing to forget Johnny's snappishness, he'd have found, come morning, that Johnny was sorry and that he was big enough to ride down and say so.

Apparently, however, judging from what he'd overheard, that pair from over at the foot of the San Paulo mountains had been in town. For reasons of their own or maybe for pure cussedness, they'd stirred Nate up.

Beating Johnny had apparently not been enough. If it had, things might still have been all right. But Nate had to go and fire those stacks too, stacks that meant wintering the herd of cattle that had come to mean so much to Will.

With hay in short supply, it was doubtful that TT would give another chance to a man who would wantonly destroy a hundred and fifty tons.

Will's jaw firmed out and anger touched his eyes. He didn't want to leave this country. He didn't want to farm. He wanted to raise cattle and he and his father already had a start. But unless something was done, and quickly too, the start would be gone by spring. Cattle that couldn't be wintered had to be sold. No matter what kind of price they brought.

Riding with Johnny and Sam all summer, Will had come to know them pretty well. He figured if he could talk his father into riding up to TT tonight and owning up to what he'd done — if he could talk his father into paying for the burned hay, then maybe Johnny and Sam could be talked into letting him have a little more — maybe enough to see the cattle through.

He whirled his horse suddenly and sank spurs into the animal's sides. Maybe the decision that he had found it so impossible to make didn't have to be made at all. Maybe he could still bring his father and TT together.

He rode hard downcountry, passing the burning stacks again on the way. The brightness of the fire was gone now and they gleamed like three enormous coals in the faint breeze blowing against them. They sent up a pillar of smoke that, in daylight, would have been seen for fifty miles.

Will rode almost excitedly through the wire gate whose location he knew so well and on toward the house. Only when he saw that it was dark did worry touch him. Still, it *was* getting late. Maybe his father had gone to bed.

He dismounted at the kitchen door and dropped the reins to the ground. He burst inside.

He went through the big kitchen, straight to the bedroom his father and mother shared. He opened the door, stared across the room at the bed. He could see his mother's shape there, blanket-wrapped, and that was all.

His voice was young and scared. "Ma! Ma!"

She stirred and sat up. "Who is it? Will?"

"Yes ma. It's me. Where's pa? Isn't he home?"

"You don't see him here do you?" Her voice held its habitual snappishness.

"No. You know where he is, ma?"

"In town, I guess. I thought you were helping bring the cattle home."

"I was. Only there's been trouble. Those three haystacks we were going to buy—" He stopped, confused, his mind racing.

"What about them? Will! Was that fire—?"

"That was what you saw. Somebody set them afire."

"Who? Who'd do an awful thing like that?"

He said, "I don't know. But I've got to find pa." He didn't want to spend any more time here. He didn't have the answers his mother was demanding.

And his father's absence scared him more than any other single thing. Because it meant his father wasn't through. It meant that somewhere out in the darkness his father, his father's neighbors and Whitey and Kiowa were riding.

He ran out, even though his mother's querulous, snappish voice followed him, questioning, demanding that he wait. He burst out the kitchen door, slamming it behind. He ran toward his horse. Frightened, the animal trotted away.

Will stopped running. He continued to advance toward the horse, speaking soothing words but seething inside.

Where could his father have gone? Who was he with and what did he hope to gain? And how could Will ever hope to find him when he hadn't the slightest idea where to begin his search?

He mounted his horse and rode out aimlessly, taking the lane that led toward the road. If his father was still in town there was nothing to worry about and no use going there. But if his father was somewhere in the darkness riding with Whitey and Kiowa and the others, then he had better find him before it was too late.

He trotted his horse up the road toward TT, uneasiness and terror gradually possessing his mind.

There was a lot of inflammatory talk in town after the fight in which Johnny Toothaker was so badly beaten and which Sam Tolle had broken up so unceremoniously. Disgruntled talk. Hate talk, led by Whitey, who held a bloody bar towel to his bleeding mouth, removing it only to curse TT at intervals. Revenge talk, led by Lou Saks, carrying his broken arm in a white cloth sling. And talk of action, led by usually quiet Kiowa.

At first it did not occur to Nate Dunn to question the motives of the three. They were saying the things that Nate, disgruntled and angry, wanted to hear.

His father's stiff-necked pride was strong in him now, untempered by his own customary reasonableness. He had gone like a beggar to Johnny Toothaker and had been contemptuously refused. Hell, the situation here on the Cottonwood was no better than the feudal system that had existed in Europe hundreds of years ago. Toothaker and Tolle were the feudal barons. Nate Dunn and his neighbors were the serfs.

An extreme comparison, but one which pleased him tonight. He had consumed more whisky than he usually did and more than he could afford, but it had left him with a feeling of recklessness foreign to him.

At last he said, this recklessness in him breaking out, "There's been a lot of goddam talk, but nothin' done. Is that all we're goin' to do? Talk?"

Kiowa's eyes brightened. "Talk ain't going to hurt either Toothaker or Tolle, that's sure. It ain't going to change anything either. In fact, if that's all you're going to do, I'm going home."

Whitey removed the bar towel to utter a stream of thick-voiced profanity. Lou Saks blustered, "I'm goin' to do something. Tonight! They gave me forty-eight hours and before that time's up I want to see them on their goddam knees!"

Uneasiness touched Nate. To quiet it, he took another drink. He asked, "What do you suggest we do?" He was looking at Kiowa as he said it, unconsciously acknowledging the still-faced man as the leader of the group.

"Refused you hay, didn't he? Make him wish he'd sold it to you."

"How?"

"Only takes one match."

For some reason the idea appealed to Nate. He was feeling badly used. He thought that having attacked Johnny and beaten him, he had spoiled his chance forever of getting the hay he needed from TT.

But he could make Johnny wish he hadn't been so damn uppity. He could make him wish he'd sold the hay. He could keep Johnny from using it himself.

That'd show TT that their neighbors had some pride. Maybe when they saw those stacks go up in smoke they'd realize you can't walk all over other men even if you have got more land and cattle and money than they have.

He quieted the deep uneasiness that struggled helplessly in the back of his mind. Enough of being walked on. Enough of being made to feel like a beggar. He got up. "Let's go then. Let's quit talking about it and get it done!"

Still that uneasiness crawled in the back of his mind. He thought of Will and resolutely put the thought away from him. If Will was such a damn good son, why wasn't he here instead of up there with the TT crew? Why wasn't he around when his father needed him?

They all filed out to their horses. Whitey and Kiowa mounted and led out.

They did not ride hard, but held their horses to a walk all the way up the long grade out of town, lifting them to a trot only when the road had leveled out.

Nate rode in front with Whitey and Kiowa. Lou Saks rode behind with two of Nate's neighbors. The rest came along behind in a straggling, uncertain group.

The cold air and the passing miles began to sober Nate long before they reached his place. His uneasiness began to grow. A chill came over him and he began to shiver in his saddle.

He knew now that he was like a train, roaring down a track at top speed toward certain destruction ahead. Yet he also knew he could neither turn off nor stop. He had set destiny in motion but he had lost control of it. He could not have stopped Whitey and Kiowa and Lou Saks now if he had tried.

A feeling of hopelessness came over him, a feeling close to despair. By refusing him hay tonight, Johnny Toothaker had completely destroyed any chance he had of wintering his herd. And if he sold the cattle, Will was sure to run away from home.

Damn Johnny! Damn the whole outfit! He whipped up his anger, discovering that it lessened his fear and helped drive away his awful feeling of despair.

They rode past his house at a steady trot, turned in at the first wire gate in TT's fence. They rode across the field and pulled up in the towering shadows of the three big stacks. Kiowa lit a match and tossed it at the foot of one of the stacks. Lou Saks and Whitey took care of the other two. Nate watched them ashamed of his relief that he had not been asked to actually set the fires himself.

Because he realized he couldn't have done it. Frugality was too deeply ingrained in him for him to countenance wanton destruction of good livestock feed.

The fires flickered feebly at the bottoms of the three tall stacks. Nate realized that even now a man could stamp them out. But he didn't move. He was scared now, scared of the avalanche of destruction he had set in motion. He looked at Kiowa's face in the mounting glare and he realized that Kiowa would shoot down the man who tried to put out the growing fires.

Flame licked up the sides of the stacks, spreading as it did. In seconds it was shooting twenty-five feet into the air.

Kiowa shouted over the mounting roar, "Let's get the hell out of here! We've got a lot of work to do!"

One man yelled, "Not me! We've done enough!"

Kiowa turned his horse. His face, even with the brilliant red light of the mounting flames on it, was cold and grayish looking. He rode to the man who had yelled and faced him. The man tried to meet his eyes and failed. Kiowa said distinctly, "We've got a lot of work to do. We're not through yet. Isn't that right, mister?"

The man tried again, stubbornly, to meet his eyes. He failed a second time and at last nodded. Kiowa shouted, "Then let's get at it!"

He turned his horse and rode away toward the road. Whitey rode beside him for several moments. They talked, but Nate didn't hear their words. When they reached the road, Whitey dropped back to close the gate and after that remained in the rear of the group.

Nate's feeling of premonition deepened. They were prisoners in this now whether all of them realized it or not. Any who tried to leave, who tried to back out and quit, would have that gunman Kiowa to reckon with.

What had begun as petulant revenge was now something much bigger than that, something that Nate felt would end in tragedy before the night was done.

All effects of the liquor he had drunk had now worn off, leaving him with a headache and a feeling of nausea.

Briefly he considered cutting away from the group, spurring his horse and riding to the TT home place to warn them. He discarded the idea almost as soon as he had it. Both Kiowa and Whitey were riding horses much faster than his own. He wouldn't get a quarter mile.

His face settled into a pattern of hopeless resignation. He and the others were a part of whatever Kiowa had in mind. It was too late to back out now.

Chapter Ten

Johnny and Sam and the crew rode into the yard at TT and headed for the corral. Johnny cut away from the others and rode directly to the house.

Robin was standing on the porch, having watched them ride in. Johnny dismounted, but before he could tie his horse, Robin reached him. Her hands gripped his arms with terrified strength. "Johnny! I saw them! I saw them riding up on the ridge to the east of here."

Johnny turned his head and bawled. "Hold it! Don't take your saddles off!"

He returned his attention to Robin. "Who did you see?"

"I don't know. But there were twelve of them. I counted. You'd just ridden down through the field toward those burning stacks.

I was standing on the porch and I saw them against the sky as they crossed the ridge."

Johnny frowned, Sam Tolle and Arleigh Peters came across the yard, leading their horses. Johnny said, "Robin saw twelve men riding up on the ridge while we were down at those burning stacks. They were heading north as they crossed the ridge."

"Then they're up to somethin' else," Sam growled.

Peters said, "The cattle."

Johnny shook his head. "I doubt it. They'd have to drive them past here to reach the left fork of the Cottonwood."

Johnny felt weak from loss of blood. His thigh, where the pitchfork tine had pierced it, throbbed steadily with excruciating pain. He felt lightheaded, as though he might fall at any time.

It seemed incredible, like a nightmare, what was happening tonight. It was as though a dam had burst, releasing the stored-up hatreds of years, hatreds he hadn't even known existed.

Sam Tolle said, "It's that pair from over at the foot of the San Paulos. An' Lou Saks."

"That's only three. Robin said twelve."

"Nine of our neighbors, then."

Peters said, "Let me take the men, Sam. We'll flush 'em out."

Johnny didn't miss the fact that Peters had asked Sam. He said, "No. Not yet. Hit that bunch in the dark and men on both sides are going to get killed."

"But — Jesus, Johnny! We ain't going to let them get away with it, are we?"

Sam was quiet. His eyes were fixed on Johnny's face, as though he were trying to read its expression in spite of the poor light coming from the open doorway of the house.

Johnny said, "They won't get away with it. We know who they are."

Sam's voice was quiet. "If it's Whitey Post an' Kiowa, we know what they want, too."

Johnny nodded. "Cattle. They didn't burn those haystacks for fun. And they wouldn't tackle anything this risky unless there was money in it for them."

Robin spoke, her voice almost breathless with fear. "They wouldn't risk it even for money as long as you and Sam—" She stopped. Johnny, close to her, could feel the shudder that ran through her. She had realizd, then, what Whitey's and Kiowa's ultimate intentions were. They intended that both Johnny and Sam should die. With ten men already in deep trouble over the burning of the stacks behind them, they were ready to stake everything on getting Johnny and Sam and driving the cattle off before any opposition got organized.

Johnny tried to guess what their next move was going to be. He sat down abruptly on the steps leading to the porch. His head swam with weakness.

Robin said worriedly, "Johnny! You ought to be in bed!"

Sam agreed, "Yeah, kid. We'll take care of this."

Johnny shook his head stubbornly. "Huh uh. I started it and I'm going to finish it. But don't let's go off half cocked. Let's figure the damn thing out. Supposing Whitey and Kiowa are planning to get rid of the two of us. What's their first move going to have to be?"

Sam didn't answer, so Johnny said, "They've got to scatter the crew, don't they? They've got to catch us alone, or almost alone."

Sam nodded, "Makes sense."

"And what's the best way to scatter the crew?"

"Burning haystacks. First at one end of the place and then—" He stopped, his eyes turning toward the north.

Johnny looked in that direction too, but he saw nothing.

Sam said, "Surely you don't think we ought to sit on our hunkers while they burn our winter feed? No sir. Not me."

"We could set us a nice little trap."

"Yeah. Sure. And how much hay do you think we'd have left by the time they took the bait?"

Peters said, "Sam, I think Johnny's right. At least part way. I think they're going to do just what he says they will. And if we want to catch 'em in the act, we'd better get going right now."

Sam teetered indecisively, plainly unable to make up his mind. Johnny opened his mouth to speak, but he never got the words spoken. One of the men, farther out in the yard, yelled, "Look! Why the dirty—!"

Johnny jumped to his feet. He staggered, recovered, and limped farther out into the yard. There was another glow in the northern sky exactly like the one they'd seen half an hour ago in the south. More haystacks were burning just as he had predicted they would.

Johnny knew he was licked before either Sam or Arleigh Peters said a word. The whole bunch of them would go storming off.

And what about the house? What about Robin? If they'd burn haystacks they'd burn buildings too if they got the chance. He didn't want to leave her here alone, but it didn't look as though he would have much choice. Besides, even Whitey and Kiowa wouldn't dare hurt her.

Sam roared, "Get your horses! Move!"

Johnny's voice was almost as loud. "Damn it, wait!"

The men halted indecisively, looking from one partner to the other and back again. Johnny faced Sam angrily. "Use your head, Sam! How far do you think you're going to get, storming around blind? You think they're going to wait for you there at the stacks they just set afire?"

"Well, maybe not. But Christ—!"

"If you've got to go, at least do it right. Spread the men out and comb the country as you go. Send two or three of them to reinforce the men with the cattle, send someone else to town to tell the sheriff what's going on."

"We'll need—"

"A hundred men won't help you if you keep them all bunched up." He was struck suddenly by the irony of this. By his own hotheadedness, characteristic of him anyway, he had stirred the whole mess up. Yet now it was he, the hotheaded one, who was counseling calm and thoughtful Sam Tolle to think first and move slowly afterward. Sam was looking at him as though he were thinking the same thing, and Johnny grinned at him. "So I must be getting old and you must be getting younger, you damn old hothead, you!"

Sam nodded. "All right, Johnny, We'll do

121

it your way."

Johnny felt all his tightened nerves go slack. For an instant, he thought he was going to pass out, but he held on and after several moments felt better.

Robin stood close beside him, watching his face. He glanced at her and grinned reassuringly, though he didn't feel very reassuring. He said, "Luke, ride in to town. Tell whoever's at the sheriff's office that we're under attack and that we're going to defend ourselves. Tell 'em if they want the law to handle this they'd better swear in a posse and get up here."

Luke swung to his horse and galloped up the lane toward the road. Johnny said, "Sam, I hate to let three men go stay with the cattle when that bunch may not even hit the cattle. Let's send one to tell the man there not to put up a scrap if they do get hit, but to come back here. Nobody can drive cattle in the dark anyway and I've got a feeling this will be over by morning."

Sam said, "That makes sense."

Johnny nodded. "All right Jess. You go. Just back off and come here if anybody jumps you."

"Sure Johnny." Jess swung to his horse and went up the lane in the direction Luke had gone.

Johnny said, "Now let's figure out what they're going to expect us to do."

Sam grinned ruefully. "Just what I'd have done. Hightail it to those burning stacks."

"Where do you figure they'll hit us next?"

"The high meadow up the draw in back of the house."

Johnny nodded. Up there were five big stacks that could be reached by skirting the edge of the big meadow north of the house. He said, "Let's ride west then. At the edge of that draw in back of the house we'll turn north and ride along the western edge of the north hayfield. We ought to meet 'em before we've gone too far."

He turned to Robin and kissed her briefly on the forehead. "I don't think they'll come here, but if they should, get out of their way. Hear?"

She nodded. She was scared — terrified — and it showed on her whitened face and in her widened eyes. Johnny said, "They won't hurt you. They're after Sam and me, not after you."

She nodded numbly. He hated to leave her this way, scared as she was. But if the attackers did hit the house any man he left with her would get killed defending it. Besides, he didn't figure any of those in the attacking party would touch her.

He swung to his horse, felt his head reel as he hit the saddle. He yelled, "Let's go!"

He and Sam thundered down through the

yard, splashed across the Cottonwood and climbed through the brushy bottom on the other side.

An odd, unexplainable worry touched his mind and for an instant he again considered sending someone back to stay with Robin. Then he gave the idea up. They needed all the men they had to fan out in a skirmish line and work upcountry through the north hayfield. They needed as many as they could get, more even than they had, to meet Whitey and Kiowa and Lou Saks and nine of TT's neighbors who were desperate now because they all faced prison for destroying TT's hay.

But as he rode, the worry deepened. He could scoff at it and tell himself it was unfounded, but he couldn't entirely drive it from his mind.

Robin watched Johnny ride away for a second time tonight, this time more terrified than she had ever been before in her life. Johnny had said the attackers wouldn't hurt her and she kept telling herself that he was right. Heavens! She knew most of them. She knew their wives and kids. She had eaten in their homes and had entertained them here.

Whatever anger they felt was directed at Johnny and Sam, not at her.

Yet that name, Kiowa, lingered in her thoughts and no matter how many times she told herself that there were probably fifty Kiowas in this state alone, she was not reassured.

For a while, she stood out in the yard staring northward at the orange glow in the sky from the burning haystacks there. She imagined the attackers riding along the western edge of the huge hayfield, intending to burn the stacks in the wide valley west of the house. She imagined Johnny and Sam and the crew, fanned out in a line up there, riding to meet them. Unconsciously, she strained her ears, listening for the sound of gunfire. Yet she knew when it came she would hear it without straining her ears. A shot echoed across this country, audible sometimes several miles away.

She didn't want to go into the house, but she forced herself. There would probably be some kind of shooting scrape up there. Someone, on one side or the other, was sure to be hurt.

It was time she stopped being a timid city girl and became a strong ranch wife. Hot water would be needed. And bandages. And towels. The men would be hungry when they returned and they'd want gallons of coffee to drink.

Until he went out on top of the mountain to start the fall roundup, Johnny had kept a cook here at the house to feed the crew. He'd taken him along to cook for the crew during roundup, and now the man was riding with Johnny and Sam and the rest of the crew. So if any food was prepared, Robin was going to have to prepare it.

She gathered clean towels and sheets with which to make bandages. She built up the fire in the enormous ranch stove until it was roaring in the flue. She put on water to heat in three big pails.

Then she made coffee, two huge graniteware pots of it. After that she went out into the meathouse, carrying a lantern, and cut about a dozen steaks off a hindquarter of beef that was hanging there.

Going back into the house, she realized that she had forgotten to be afraid. And yet, her ears stayed tuned nervously for the sound of shots.

She put the steaks in the kitchen, then went out again to the potato cellar. She gathered about ten pounds of potatoes and, carrying them in her apron, returned to the house. Almost absently she dumped them into a pan, poured water over them, then began peeling them.

This afternoon there had been a time when she hated Johnny for doubting her, for believing the worst of her. But that was gone.

However wrong he had been, tonight he needed her. She would be here when he came – to feed him, to dress his wounds if he was hurt, to love him. She knew his knowledge that she was here made easier the things he might have to do.

She finished slicing the potatoes and laid them aside. There was now nothing left to do before they came. She wandered through the house, beginning to grow uneasy again.

Resolutely, she returned to the kitchen. If she didn't keep busy, she was going to go crazy with fear. She got a huge mixing bowl, flour and other ingredients and began to bake a cake, smiling to herself as she did. Johnny might think she was crazy when he got back, and maybe she was. But being busy was the only thing that helped.

For somewhere in the back of her mind that name, Kiowa, remained. And though she was able to put her terror aside, it did not disappear.

Chapter Eleven

The night was dark and a thin layer of clouds covered the stars. Diffused starlight lightened them enough to make the horizons on all sides of the galloping party of horsemen visible against the clouds.

Behind Johnny, the Cottonwood rustled along between its brush-grown banks. Usually at this time of year it carried three times the water it did now. This lack of water had sharply reduced the size of the country's crop of hay. TT's crop was nearer normal than that of the smaller ranchers, the reason being that they had the first water right out of the Cottonwood, but even TT had planned to sell off as many cattle as were saleable. And, in spite of Johnny's refusal of Nate Dunn's request, they'd fully intended to share what hay they had with as many of their neighbors as needed it.

Now it was too late for that. Several hundred tons of it had already been destroyed. Wantonly. Without good cause. And both TT and the smaller ranchers would have to live with the loss.

After leaving the bed of the Cottonwood, the party climbed sharply for a quarter mile through a deep, brush-choked ravine, the bottom of which carried the trickle they called Tolle Creek. Then, with a suddeness that somehow always pleased Johnny, they left the ravine and climbed out onto the enormous hay meadow.

It stretched to the west for about six miles, almost flat but gently sloping toward the house. In places it narrowed to a few hundred yards, in others widened to a mile or two.

Johnny heard a big bunch of deer spook away from the mounted men. Then Sam Tolle turned right and headed north along the edge of the meadow.

The others followed. Johnny was dizzy and his leg sent shafts of pain shooting into his groin with every jolting movement of his horse. He gritted his teeth and kept up, but he didn't forge ahead.

They skirted the bottom of the Tolle Creek meadow for about a half mile, rode through a quarter-mile stretch of high sagebrush, then entered the north hayfield at its upper edge.

Sam Tolle hauled up and Johnny caught up with him. The others sat their fidgeting horses silently. Every man had his ears tuned for the sound of hoofs.

Sam said softly, "Wonder if we missed 'em. Maybe they're already past here and on their way up Tolle Creek."

Johnny said, "Figure it. Those stacks they set are better than four miles from the house. They couldn't ride that far while we were coming from the house. Not even with the start they had. But they can't be far. They can't be very far if my guess was right."

"And they haven't stopped to fire any others on the way or we'd have seen them."

Johnny said, "Let' spread out — about a hundred yards between each man, and ride north from here. They can't get through without somebody seein' them."

Almost silently the men moved away as Sam Tolle softly called their names, riding directly into the darkness of the silent meadow, their only sound that of their horses' hoofs rustling the stubble of the hay. Sam put Arleigh Peters almost in the center of the line, with Jake McRae on his right, Dave Dunklee on his left. Sam rode out after Dave and Johnny rode along the upper edge of the meadow in the shadow of the brush.

They rode slowly, almost silently, frequently glancing to right or left to check the position of the men riding next to them. You could see a man at a hundred yards but not much farther than that.

As Johnny rode, tension coupled with regret mounted in him. He realized that this had gone too far to end without bloodshed or even death. When the two forces came together there would be bullets exchanged and even in the dark it was inevitable that some of them would find their marks.

His horse paced along slowly. The weakness Johnny had felt earlier was gone now, driven away by the tension and urgency of the moment.

He could see Sam dimly in the darkness. Horse and rider were only a blacker, moving mass against the blackness of the meadow. Beyond Sam he could see nothing.

He glanced around at the house. Its lighted windows shone like beacons through the brush and trees that lined the creek.

He thought he heard hoofs and drew his horse to a momentary halt to listen. He opened his mouth to shout.

A shot flared, orange and wicked, ahead of

him and to his right.

Johnny snatched his gun from its holster and thumbed back the hammer. His spurs touched his horse's sides and the animal leaped ahead. Another glance to his right showed him Sam, galloping too.

He heard Sam's yell, "Johnny! The rest of you! Hold your positions! Don't let 'em through!"

Johnny switched his glance straight ahead. He saw a dark mass — two of them — thundering toward him.

He snapped a shot at one, holding his point of aim low so that he would hit the horse instead of the man. In his mind he was still making excuses for these neighbors of his that he knew so well.

The horse stumbled and pitched forward. Man and horse went rolling past Johnny's galloping mount. He saw the bright flare of a gun ahead of him and almost in his face and fired a second time. Then this one was past him too and there was nothing at all ahead.

He whirled his horse, rearing, in the darkness. All along the line shots were flaring now, blossoming like flowers of death in the blackness of the night. Men were shouting, horses nickering shrilly. There were the sounds of plunging hoofs, of straining girths and stirrup leathers, occasionally a curse. In the melee friend was indistinguishable from foe.

Johnny galloped back in the direction he had come, searching for the two who had gone on past. He saw a horseman fighting a bucking horse and yelled, "Sam?" his finger light upon his trigger. He got no answer, and fired immediately. The horse stopped bucking and bolted past him straight into the high brush of the hillside above the meadow. Johnny could hear him crashing through it, the sounds diminishing. That one was out of the fight. His bullet must have stung the horse to make him run like that. And the fight would be over before his rider brought him under control again.

The one he had downed — he could hear the horse thrashing on the ground to his left. He rode that way, with a glance over his shoulder to be sure no more of them were coming at him from behind.

The shooting had died to a desultory exchange. Somewhere out in the meadow a wounded horse was wheezing through a severed windpipe. He heard Sam yell, "Johnny! You all right?" with worry strong in his voice.

Johnny didn't answer immediately, for the man he had downed was close, he knew. Until he located him he didn't particularly care to identify himself.

But when he heard Sam riding toward him he yelled, "All right, Sam! Stay where you are! There's one of 'em down over here and I haven't found him yet!"

Flame lanced at him from close to the ground. The bullet whined past his head less than a yard away, making a quick, furiously whistling sound as it passed.

Johnny swung his gun and fired instantly at the flare. Then he was past the man, turning, fighting his frightened horse.

He saw the man rise from the ground and run, run north in the direction from which he had come only minutes before. Johnny could have ridden him down and killed him with ease. Instead he held his plunging horse still with a hard, brutal hand on the reins. The man disappeared into the meadow's dark reaches.

Johnny yelled, "All right Sam! All right! He's gone."

The meadow was suddenly silent except for the hard breathing of men, except for the thrashing sounds of the horse Johnny had downed and the wheezing one farther out. He rode toward the place Sam's voice had come from last, yelling, "Where you at, Sam?"

"Here. Over here. I think somebody's hurt."

"They gone?"

"They're gone. The dirty sons-of-bitches!"

"Who's hurt?"

"I don't know. Somebody over on my right."

Johnny paced his horse toward the sound of Sam's voice and reached him a few seconds later. Abreast, they rode on, pulling up when they heard a man groan softly from the ground. Johnny swung down and followed suit. Sam called softly, "Who is it?"

The voice that answered came through teeth clenched tight against pain. "It's me. The bastards got me in the leg."

Arleigh Peters. Johnny said, "Lie still. We'll get some light.

He yelled, "Jake!" but got no answer and felt suddenly as though a cold hand had touched his spine. He yelled, "Dave!" and waited, his breathing stilled.

The answer came immediately and Johnny's breath sighed out. He shouted, "Take someone with you. Get to the house and get a lantern. Send it out here and then hitch up a wagon as fast as you can."

"Sure Johnny. Is it Peters?"

"Yeah. And Jake too, I'm afraid. At least he didn't answer me."

He heard three of the men gallop away toward the house. He knelt beside Peters and struck a match. Peters' leg was soaked with blood between the knee and hip. There was a stain of it spreading on the ground.

Sam already had his knife in his hand. He knelt beside Johnny but Johnny said, "Wait. I'll strike another match."

He dropped the one he had and struck a fresh one. Sam slit Peters' pants leg from knee to hip, then slit it crossways so that he could peel it back and expose the wound. Johnny's match died.

He struck another. It was a nasty wound and bleeding freely, but he saw no bone splinters in it.

He heard someone yell, "What the hell—" and saw another match flare farther out in the meadow. The man holding the match knelt. The match went out and his voice came, shocked and soft, from the darkness. "It's Jake McRae! He's dead!"

A kind of empty sickness touched Johnny's stomach. And now, at last, his anger stirred and grew. These were neighbors that he and Sam had fought tonight. These were men he understood, who'd had his sympathies. But not any more. Not now. Because these same men had wounded Peters and killed Jake McRae. They were outlaws now, to be hunted down and shot.

He wondered whether he should tie his shirt around Peters' wound, but decided against it at least until the man returned with the lantern.

Maybe he'd think to bring bandages too. He struck another match and looked at the foreman's wound again. It was bleeding freely but not in spurts. Apparently, then, the bullet had cut no arteries. Peters was in no immediate danger of bleeding to death.

He rose to his feet. "I'll take a look at Jake. Maybe—"

He walked across the black hayfield to where two or three of the men were standing. "Where's Jake?"

One of them said, "Over here, Johnny," and led the way.

Johnny followed. He knelt beside the still form on the ground. He struck a match. In its light he picked up Jake McRae's wrist.

He felt for pulse, but could find none. He laid his head on Jake's deep chest and listened for heartbeat. There was none. Nor was there any rise and fall to Jake's chest. Jake was dead.

He knelt there, stunned. Jake had been with Sam Tolle when he picked Johnny off that freight. Jake had stuck up for Johnny lots of times during those first few years whenever Johnny would have a spat with Sam.

A gruff and sometimes blustering oldster, Jake was TT ranch to Johnny as much as any other single person or thing. It wasn't going to be the same with him gone.

Damn Nate Dunn! Damn that trashy pair from over in the San Paulo mountains! Damn Lou Saks!

It had been a long time since Johnny had felt like crying, but he did right now. Tears burned behind his eyes and his throat felt choked.

He stood up. "Where the hell's that lantern an' wagon? Damn it!"

Someone said, "Here they come, Johnny."

He looked toward the house, then right of the house toward the foot of the Tolle Creek meadow. He saw a brightly flickering light, that of the lantern, coming unsteadily toward him. He heard the pounding hoofs of the heavy wagon team, heard the rattle of chain tugs, the banging of wagon floorboards, the yelling of the driver as he urged the team into a reckless run over the uneven ground.

The wagon hit a ditch and bounded high with a resounding crash. The man with the lantern went down, but the lantern didn't break.

Then the wagon was pulling up beside Arleigh Peters and the man with the lantern was leaping down.

He thrust a bundle of sheet bandages into Johnny's hands. "Robin said to tie it up with this and bring him in. She'll have everything ready for you as soon as you get there."

Sam Tolle gently raised Arleigh Peters' leg

and Johnny wound bandages tightly around it. Then, between them, they lifted him to the bed of the wagon into which half a dozen pitchfork loads of hay and some blankets had been thrown. Johnny growled, "Don't drive goin' back like you did getting here," and turned away.

The wagon moved off toward the house, being driven with extreme care. Johnny caught up his horse and led him to where Jake McRae's body lay. He lifted the old man and laid him carefully across the saddle. He said, "Two of you walk alongside and steady him."

Then he led away, walking, toward the house. His face was set in grim and angry lines. He had a score to be settled. He intended to see that it was settled before the sun came up tomorrow.

Chapter Twelve

Will Dunn stopped at the wide pole gate where the TT lane led west from the main road. He stared down at the lighted windows of the house, a bit of wistfulness in his face.

He wanted to go down there and be with the TT crew, with Johnny and with Sam. He felt, somehow, as though he belonged with them. When the night was over, they probably wouldn't want him with them any more. He would be an enemy, just as his father was.

He turned his head resolutely away, touched his horse's sides with his heels and rode on up the road.

A mile above the house he turned in at a wire gate and closed it carefully behind him. Mounted again, he set off across the enormous hayfield, heading north.

He saw the glow in the northern sky at about the time Sam and Johnny did and pulled his horse to a sudden halt.

This was exactly what he had feared most when he found that his father was not at home. The first hay burnings had not been the last. Whitey and Kiowa and Lou Saks and his father and the others meant to go on with it throughout the night.

That Toothaker and Tolle would fight, Will did not doubt for a moment. With each successive burning they would become more enraged, until they would shoot to kill everyone they saw on TT who did not belong.

Will's horse was tired and stood patiently, his head down. And Will sat his saddle as though frozen, his mind racing as he tried to guess what the bunch his father was riding with would do next.

Whitey and Kiowa. What did they want or expect to gain from this? Revenge? He doubted it, doubted if they had ever had any dealings with TT to give them reason for revenge.

Profit then. In some way they expected to gain something from leading these wantonly destructive attacks.

The only profit Will could think of was the TT cattle, even now corralled at Three Mile Corral, three miles above the Cottonwood and

Brush Creek forks.

He frowned. How did they expect to get those cattle out of the country? They couldn't while Johnny and Sam were around to stop them.

Will's frown deepened, and his eyes turned scared. He could reach only one conclusion. Kiowa and Whitey intended that both Johnny and Sam should die.

And Lou Saks. Johnny had beaten him, broken his arm, and driven him off the place. Lou Saks might be the tool Whitey and Kiowa intended to use to accomplish their purpose.

The glow in the northern sky was much brighter now in spite of the fact that it was more than three miles away. He could see great clouds of smoke rolling skyward, lighted and turned red by the blazing fire below.

No use riding to those burning stacks. His father and the others would not be there. Where, then, could he look?

First, he supposed, he would have to try and guess what they intended to do next. Attack the house? He shook his head. He doubted if any of that bunch had the courage for an all-out attack against TT.

More haystacks then, with the ultimate objective of scattering TT's forces to guard the remaining unburned ones. Once TT's crew was scattered, then the attack upon the house would come.

He wondered where the next burning would be. The first had been at TT's southern boundary, the second almost as far north as they could go. The third, then, had to come either on the south again or west, up Tolle Creek.

He put his horse into motion, riding west across the broad hayfield. Perhaps he could intercept them as they headed along the western boundary of this field.

He rode at a walk, carefully and almost silently. He didn't want to run headlong into any group of TT riders because he knew that by now they'd be ready to shoot first and ask questions afterward.

He was nearly across the field, in fact he could see the dark line of brush that marked its western edge, when the first shot flared wildly ahead of him.

He hauled his horse to an immediate halt. A feeling of despair touched his mind and something cold lay against the base of his spine. He was too late. An open clash had come and there was no longer any hope that he could do anything to ward it off.

Not that he'd ever had much chance, he thought. He doubted if his father, having gone this far, would listen to reason now. He knew he would not be able to dissuade a couple of hardcases like Kiowa and Whitey Post.

Frozen, unable to do anything but watch, he sat his horse while the battle flared and grew, while it died to a desultory exchange of shots and finally stopped. He heard the enraged shouts from the TT crew. He heard the names, Peters and McRae, and knew that TT had been badly hurt.

He hoped bitterly that the other side had been hurt as badly. He found himself hoping that his father had been hurt enough to put him out of the fight.

Because it wasn't over. The lines were drawn and the fight would continue throughout the night until either one side or the other was licked.

Will felt nearer to tears than he had for years. What could he do? Where could he go? And how could he stop something as awesome and terrible as this battle going on here in the black and fragrant hay meadows of TT ranch?

Perhaps he couldn't. But he knew one thing. Never would he be able to live with himself if he didn't try.

With his mind made up, with his face white and set, his mouth held firm because of its dismaying tendency to tremble, he rode north in the wake of the attackers, who had now retired.

He rode slowly, deliberately, knowing that those he approached would be wary of pursuit by TT and likely to shoot at sounds and movements before they knew for sure what made them.

Straight toward the burning haystacks he rode, quartering back and forth in the hopes that he would be able to outline the shapes of the men he sought and their horses against the light before they could see or hear him.

He had gone for perhaps a mile and was dropping down into a kind of hollow in the field, when a rifle cracked wickedly on his right.

The bullet missed, but not by very far. Will dived out of his saddle and hit the ground sprawling. Shaking so badly he could hardly open his mouth, he yelled, "Don't! It's me! It's Will Dunn!"

He heard his father's bellow, a worried, anguished cry, "Hold it! That's my kid out there!"

Will stayed on the ground, though his horse had moved away in the direction from which he'd come. After a few moments he heard footsteps in the hay stubble and the scarcely recognizable voice of his father. "Will! You hurt?"

Will scrambled to his feet. "Huh uh. I ain't hurt."

"What you doing here? Dammit, you're supposed to be home. You don't have to hang around TT when you ain't working for them."

"What are you doing here, pa? That's what I want to know."

"You never mind that, boy. I'm doin' what I got to do. You just hightail it for home right now, before I tan you."

"That hay, pa. All that hay! Why'd you burn it when you knew we had to have it or sell the cattle?"

"Don't you back talk me! Just hightail it for home."

"Not yet, pa. Not until—"

The thick, pain-filled voice of Whitey Post interrupted as the man approached the pair. "What's goin' on here? Why all the goddam talk?"

Nate turned. "It's my boy. But he's goin' home."

"No I ain't, pa. I ain't goin' nowhere without you. What you're doin' is wrong. It's awful wrong. There's two men shot back there, men I like an' been ridin' with. Jake McRae an' Arleigh Peters."

Nate's voice was almost as thick as Whitey's, but from another cause. "Bad?"

"When you're shot, pa, it's always bad, ain't it?"

146

Whitey's voice again, this time heavy with suspicion. "Is this kid a TT man?"

Nate said nervously, "He's been ridin' with them because our cattle was pooled with theirs."

The others, including Kiowa and Lou Saks, had all approached the sounds of argument and now grouped themselves around the three. There was very little light, just that from the glow in the sky to northward. But when you know men as well as Will knew these, you could recognize them in any kind of light.

Kiowa was the stranger and because he was, Will knew him too.

Nate's nervousness was obviously increasing. "You git for home, boy. I'll be there after a while."

"And what then, pa? You think you ain't going to have to answer for what you done tonight?"

"Answer? Answer? They'll come to terms before we're through."

"No pa. They'll fight to the last man and you know they will."

"Then we'll fight too."

"What for? What are you fighting *for?*"

"You shut your mouth. I'm your pa! You're either for me or against me. And I reckon right now you're going to have to take your pick."

Kiowa's ugly voice broke in, "Shut up, the both of you! We got work to do an' no damn time to stand here jawin'."

Nate swung his head. *"You* shut up!"

He stared at Will again. Kiowa took a step closer to him. Will felt the iciness in his stomach turn into a hard, cold ball. The words were hard for Will to say, but there were no others he could say. "I guess I got to leave you pa. I guess—" His throat choked up and he couldn't finish. He turned away, looking for his horse.

Kiowa's harsh voice cut through the night. "Wait a minute, you little bastard! If you think I'm going to let you run back to TT and tell 'em where we are and who we are, then you're crazy!"

Will didn't turn. He wanted to run. That voice scared him and so did the threat it held.

Nate growled angrily, "Let him go. To hell—"

"No! Kid!"

Will turned. There was a prickly feeling at the base of his neck. There was tension in him so strong it was nearly intolerable. And there was another feeling — a terrifying one — that he was going to die.

He carried a gun; he'd bought it this spring when he started riding for TT. But he couldn't use it against a man. He knew he could never use it against a man.

He said, "I'll tell 'em all right. I'll tell 'em right where you are and who you are and they'll clean you out pretty fast once they know that. The whole bunch of you better scatter and go on home because you ain't likely to get another chance."

It was a long speech for Will and a breathless one. He stood there panting afterward and waiting — for what he knew Kiowa was going to do.

His father's voice was softer, calmer than it had been before. "Go home, Will. I'm coming along myself right soon."

Will didn't turn. He knew it was too late now for that. He knew, even if his father did not. He saw the swift movement of Kiowa's hand, saw the bright flare from the muzzle of Kiowa's gun.

It was like a mule kicking him squarely in the chest. A hard blow — a tremendous one, that flung him back and down. Not until he struck the ground did pain come but it came then, more terrible than anything he had ever experienced before. He began to cough on the blood that was flooding his throat. He felt his father's arms around his body. His father was holding him close against his thick, deep chest as he often had when Will was a little boy. And his father was crying; his body was wracked with tortured, spasmodic sobs.

This was dying, but Will was too stunned to realize it. His eyes were open, seeing the ring of dark shapes standing around him and looking down. Then those shapes began to blur and fade until there was nothing left but blackness with clouds of fog swirling through it.

The last thing he felt was the frantic strength of his father's arms, holding him as though some physical presence was trying to snatch Will from him. The last thing he heard was his father's voice, his anguished weeping.

There was nothing, then, for Will was dead.

Nate Dunn held the still, limp body of his son for a long, long time. Then he stood up, his son's body dangling from his arms. His first conscious thought was surprise at how light Will was, how small. It had been a long time since Nate thought of Will as being small. Will had become a man too soon. And he had died too soon.

The others, Nate's neighbors, stood stunned by the tragedy, unable to move or speak. Kiowa still held his gun in his hand. There was the faint, acrid smell of powdersmoke lingering in the air.

Nate wordlessly handed the body of his son to Dewey Roark. Turning, he was like a tiger released from his cage. His face was twisted and his eyes blazed red. He launched himself at Kiowa.

Kiowa's gun roared a second time, but it did not save him. Nate's body struck him and knocked him sprawling fifteen feet away.

Nate fell short of his prey and did not get up. But he crawled. Tortuously, dead but unwilling to admit it until he had reached the killer of his son, he crawled.

Kiowa got up. Panting, he stared at the man crawling toward him, looking up with such undying hatred in his eyes. Deliberately he shot again, then as Nate Dunn toppled, swung the gun to cover the others, whom Whitey Post was already threatening with his rifle. "That's enough! Enough, you hear? I killed those two and if I have to I'll kill some more. What the hell's the matter with you anyway? Don't you know it's too damn late to quit? You're outlaws, every one of you! You're candidates for a hangman's noose. You got only one choice an' that's to go on!"

He was screaming at them, showing more emotion than he had ever shown before.

His voice dropped, but his eyes still blazed

at them. "Get your horses and let's get on with this. Anyone that tries to run will get it in the back!"

Chapter Thirteen

It was a grim procession that headed back toward the house at TT ranch. The wagon went ahead, rattling and jolting in spite of the care exercised by Dave Dunklee who was driving.

Johnny followed, leading Jake's horse, and a man walked on each side of the horse, steadying Jake's body so that it would not fall.

In the rear came Sam and the rest of the crew, their anger, as evidenced by their talk, smoldering and growing with every step they took.

Back through the north hayfield they went, through the brushy wasteland that separated it from the Tolle Creek meadow, thence across the lower end of that and back into the bottom and across the creek.

Johnny heard the first distant shot and stopped to listen, but heard nothing further after that. Puzzling, he went on and then, later, heard two more shots and then another.

They were fighting among themselves, he supposed, and he hoped they were. But even if they fought it out among themselves and scattered they would not escape TT's vengeance for this night's work. The burning of haystacks might be forgiven if restitution were made. But murder — that was something else again.

The wagon drove up the grade from the creek into the yard. Johnny led Jake McRae's horse to the bunkhouse and eased Jake's body down and carried it inside. He laid Jake in his bunk, straightened him out and folded his hands on his chest. Then he drew a blanket up to cover Jake's dead face.

There was a kind of ache in his chest as he turned and went outside again. An ache of loss.

He crossed the yard to the house. Sam had already sent someone to town after Doc Peabody.

Not too many men were left. Arleigh Peters was laid up and Jake McRae was dead. Two men had been sent to town, one after the sheriff and one for Doc. A man had been sent to reinforce the man who was already guarding the cattle at Three Mile Corral. Lou Saks was riding with the enemy. That left only Johnny and Sam and three others. Five. And Robin had counted twelve crossing the ridge to the east of the house.

How many had been hurt badly enough to put them out of the fight? How many killed or hurt in the subsequent exchange of shots which could only have meant a fight among themselves?

He didn't know. But the odds were probably at least two to one against TT.

Not that it would matter. He didn't care what the odds were. TT was going to win.

He went inside the house quietly. He closed the door behind him.

Sam Tolle was waiting, pacing back and forth. He nodded toward the first floor bedroom he occupied himself. "Robin's in there with him taking care of his leg."

"She – hell Sam, she can't–"

Sam grinned wryly at him. "Can't she? That's a woman, Johnny. That's a real woman. Go see for yourself."

Johnny opened the door and stuck his head inside. Peters was out cold and there was a strong smell of whiskey in the air, a half empty bottle on the nightstand. Robin was just finishing a neat white bandage on his leg.

She looked around, smiled wanly at Johnny.

"It missed the bone and the arteries too. He'll be all right until the doctor comes."

Johnny nodded and Robin went on with her work, speaking over her shoulder now. "There's food in the kitchen. Take the men and Sam and go out there and eat it."

Johnny grinned. "Yes ma'am." He closed the door quietly behind him. He looked at Sam. "I was wrong. She can."

Sam returned his grin. Johnny went to the door and called to the three crewmen waiting outside. "Robin's cooked a meal. Come on and eat."

They filed inside and followed Johnny to the kitchen. For a while there was silence as they washed, seated themselves and began to eat. Then Sam Tolle said, "What now, Johnny?"

Johnny said, "We find them. And the only way I know of doing that is to patrol the ranch. We'll have to split up because there aren't many of us left. Just ride careful, all of you. We don't want anybody else getting hurt. If you locate 'em, fire three quick shots into the air. The rest of us will come running."

"How about Robin?"

"I'll leave Dave Dunklee here with her."

Robin's voice spoke sharply from the door. "You will not! I'm perfectly capable of taking care of myself and you need every man you've got."

Sam grinned at Johnny. "Didn't I tell you?"

Robin asked, "Tell him what?"

"I told him he had himself a wife."

Robin flushed with pleasure. She fled through the door, muttering something about seeing how Mr. Peters was.

Johnny finished and drained his coffee cup. He got to his feet. "I don't like leaving her, but I don't suppose even Kiowa or Whitey Post would be low enough to hurt a woman."

He shaped a cigarette and lighted up. "Sam, let's you and me and Dave take the north hayfield. Julius can take Tolle Creek and Frank the south hayfield. If we haven't found anything an hour from now, we'll all come back here."

Sam and the other three got to their feet. They filed out the door. Johnny said, "I'll be out in a minute."

He was feeling a heavy weight of responsibility — Peters' wound, Jake McRae's death. If he hadn't behaved like a jealous fool, none of this would have happened.

It didn't help to tell himself that all this hadn't come out of a simple refusal of Nate Dunn's request for hay. It hadn't come out of his fight with Lou Saks or his show of bad temper in town. It had been here all the time, smoldering like a coal, waiting only for wind to fan it into a blaze.

Kiowa and Whitey Post had been waiting for years, probably for a chance to steal the TT beef herd. Fear had held them back until now, and TT's quarrel with its neighbors had only provided the opportunity they had been waiting for.

He went into the living room, found Robin just coming out of the bedroom door. She said softly, "He's still sleeping. The shock, I suppose, and the whisky I made him drink."

Johnny crossed to her. "I'm going out again now. We're going to try and find that bunch."

Her face was pale, her eyes scared. But she smiled at him, though a forced and difficult smile it was. "All right Johnny. I'll take good care of Mr. Peters until the doctor comes."

"I know you will." He stood for a moment looking quietly down at her. Then he said hoarsely, "I never knew, I never realized – I thought I loved you before but that was pretty puny compared to the way I feel right now."

He saw a shine of tears touch her eyes. Then his arms were around her and her face was hidden against his chest. Her body trembled for several moments and then stopped. She pushed him away. "They're waiting for you, Johnny. Good luck."

Tears still brightened her eyes. But her smile

was strong and not as forced as it had been before. Johnny said, "Sam was right. I've got myself a wife."

He turned and strode to the door. He went through it without looking back.

She'd said nothing about the odds, though he knew she'd been very conscious of them. She'd said nothing about being afraid even though she was plainly terrified. She'd said nothing about doubting her ability to hold down the fort until the doctor came, though this doubt had been very plain in her. She hadn't even cautioned Johnny to be careful when it was obvious his safety was the chief cause of her concern. She had the kind of courage seldom found even in men and almost never found in women.

Johnny's chest felt tight. When tonight was over – He said hoarsely as he swung to the back of his horse, "Let's go, Sam."

He and Sam and Dave Dunklee rode north into the big hayfield. Julius Gardner rode west alone. Frank rode away to the south.

Once through the fence they separated, riding at a slow, slow walk so as not to make any noise. Sam rode on Johnny's left, Dave on his right, but because of the size of the field, both were too far away to be either seen or heard.

Johnny tried to recall from which direction

those shots had come, without success. He tried to guess how far away they had been, with little better luck. A fourth of the way to the burning stacks, he supposed. A mile or less from the house.

He doubted if they'd group out in the open field. If they were out here, then, they would probably head for a clump of scrub-oak out in the middle of the field that had never been cleared away.

It was about two acres in size, occupying a high place in the field that was both rocky and difficult to irrigate, which accounted for the fact that it had never been cleared.

He turned his horse slightly to head for it, trying as he rode to guess exactly what had happened in the opposing group after the clash in which Peters had been hurt and McRae killed.

They had undoubtedly pulled back; they had been driven back. He doubted if they'd had any serious casualties, however, because they'd had no time for removing wounded or dead and none had been left at the scene of the battle.

Having pulled back, Johnny believed they had argued among themselves. Dunn and the rest of TT's neighbors had probably tried to back out, appalled at what they had done. Kiowa and Whitey and Lou had refused to let them quit. The argument had ended in gunfire and had, no doubt, resulted in one or more of the group being hurt or killed.

All this must have taken time, perhaps as much time as Johnny and his crew had taken bringing Peters and McRae in and eating Robin's supper afterward. Now they would be trying to decide what their next move would be, unless they had already decided it.

Of one thing Johnny was sure. None of the bunch would or could quit now. The thing had gone too far. Only by destroying TT could the opposition hope to win. And as long as either Johnny Toothaker or Sam Tolle lived, TT would be a force to reckon with.

Ahead, now, he could see the darker mass in the field that was the scrub-oak clump. He strained his eyes, trying to see some light, but he saw nothing at all. He slowed his horse until the animal scarcely moved.

A hundred yards from the nearest trees he stopped. He raised his head and checked the wind. It was blowing from the east, across the field and would neither carry the scent of Johnny's horse to those of the attacking force, nor the scent of theirs to his.

He dismounted while still fifty yards short of the nearest trees and led his horse the rest of the way. He tied him at the edge of the clump to a scrubby tree standing a few feet away from the rest. Then, afoot, he started through the tangled, twisted trees.

Less than halfway through he heard voices, and after that proceeded with even more caution than before. He continued until he could make out their words.

Frank Dulane was speaking, but not in his usual intemperate way. "We're all fools, Whitey. If we don't back off from this thing we're going to end up with our necks in a noose right along with Kiowa. I say we'd all better get the hell out of here while we've got a chance."

And Whitey's voice, thick and hard to understand because of his lost front teeth. "Shut up. Kiowa said to wait and by God we'll wait. Unless you want a taste of what Nate Dunn and that kid of his got."

Frozen and silent, his mind racing, Johnny knew he had made a mistake, perhaps a disasterous one. Kiowa, the most deadly of the lot, wasn't with the bunch. And there was only one place he could have gone.

He began to back away, wanting to whirl and run, to claw aside the tangled trees.

Robin was there, alone in the house or virtually alone because Arleigh Peters was unconscious. And Kiowa had left the group in the thicket—

A branch cracked under Johnny's foot and

the voices stopped. He cursed softly under his breath, but he didn't stop. He didn't dare.

Speed was essential now. He had assumed before that Kiowa wouldn't hurt a woman but now he wasn't sure. He remembered the man, remembered his eyes and the impassive mold of his face. People said Kiowa had Indian blood and it was probably true.

He had killed Nate Dunn and Nate Dunn's boy. Johnny had to assume that was what had happened from Whitey's cryptic reference to their fate. He was in as deep as a man can get.

But if he touched Robin — Johnny threw caution to the winds and began to run. If Kiowa touched Robin he'd follow the man ten thousand miles if he had to. And kill him in a way that an Indian would understand.

He heard a shout behind him, a quick shout of alarm. He heard the sounds of many feet crashing through the thicket behind him.

Unheeding, he burst out into the open. He thought of firing three shots and snatched his gun from its holster before he changed his mind. The danger wasn't here, in these frightened ranchers, in this pain-crazed outlaw, in the vengeance-hungry Lou Saks. The danger was there at the house. Kiowa was the dangerous one.

He had to slow his pace to a walk or give his location away. Walking fast, he reached his horse, untied him and swung to the saddle with a leap. He sank his spurs into the horse's sides even as he yanked his head around.

Another shout lifted behind him and a gun flared in the inky dark. Then Johnny was away, raking his horse mercilessly with his spurs and leaning low over his neck.

The house lay more than a mile ahead of him. And he knew how much could happen while a man was riding a mile.

He was sweating heavily; but cold as well. His wounds and weariness forgotten, he rode as he had never ridden before.

Chapter Fourteen

The emotion Kiowa felt as he stared down at the bodies of Will and Nate Dunn was not regret or shame. It was anger.

For a spur of the moment business, he had planned this well. From the haystacks down at Nate Dunn's fence, the burning of which had immediately drawn the TT crew, to the burning of the second group of stacks at the north end of TT, things had gone exactly as he had planned.

Then something had gone wrong. Instead of splitting their forces to guard the remaining groups of stacks scattered over their vast network of hayfields, TT had intercepted the raiding party between the blazing north stacks and the lower end of the Tolle Creek meadow.

That had been setback number one, a serious one because it had resulted in some injuries and maybe even deaths among the TT crewmen thus stiffening their resistance. It had demoralized the small ranchers upon whom Kiowa had to rely and had forced him to change his plan.

There now seemed to be little chance of catching either Johnny or Sam Tolle in a position where he could be killed. Nor, after this episode, could he really rely on the small ranchers he had left. They might go along with him; they could be forced into that. But they could not be relied upon as fighters.

He glowered savagely at the cowed ranchers. There had been some light while the stacks were blazing in spite of the fact that they were three miles away. Now that the light from them was fading it was more difficult to see the men. Even so, he could tell by the way they stood that they were both rebellious and sullen. They knew that they had been fools. They knew that Kiowa was using them and they had reached the point where they were no longer willing to go on getting in deeper and deeper. They realized now that but one course remained for them, that being to surrender themselves and take what was coming to them, whatever it happened to be.

As a fighting force, then, they were useless. Unpalatable as that admission might be, Kiowa had to accept it. Which left him with only Whitey and Saks, both of whom were crazed with hate and pain and incapable of either cool judgment or effective action.

Stealing the TT herd was therefore out of the question now. Not only that. Remaining in the country was out of the question as far as he was concerned. He'd be caught and jailed and hanged for the double killing of Will and Nate. But how to salvage something? How to get out of the country with something to show for his efforts and the risks he had taken?

He stared at the cowed ranchers contemptuously. He said, "We can't stay here. There's a pocket of scrub-oak farther north in the middle of this field. Get on up there and wait. I'll see if there's anything I can do."

Nobody moved. Kiowa snarled, "Move, you yellow-bellies! Move! Before I lose my temper good. You think I'd hesitate about killing you? They sure as hell can't hang me more than once!"

That broke them up. They mounted their horses and turned north toward the scrub-oak thicket in the middle of the field. Whitey and Lou stayed with Kiowa until they started, then rode with him behind them. Kiowa said, "Hold 'em there until I get back. This hasn't turned out the way we planned, but maybe there's still something that can be done."

Neither Whitey nor Lou replied. Kiowa realized that they were frightened too.

His mouth turned down at the corners again. They'd be a hell of a sight more scared if they knew he had no intention of coming back here unless he had to come.

For another plan was growing in his mind. This time of year the amount of cash on hand at TT might not be as great as it would be later in the fall. But it might be enough. There ought to be a couple of thousand there at the very least. If he could get that, and a fresh horse — if he could figure something that would keep TT too busy to pursue — then he might get out of this with a whole skin yet.

He swung his horse and headed across the dark hay meadow toward the winking lights in the TT house.

Damn! For three years now he and Whitey Post had sat it out in that crummy shack over there at the foot of the San Paulo range. Sure, they'd been hiding out over another business down in New Mexico. But it hadn't been fun and they hadn't had to stay three years. They'd been trying to figure some way of getting hold of that fat TT beef herd and the money it would bring. But at times he'd got so sick of Whitey's complaining that he wanted to kill the man.

Tonight he'd thought he'd found the way. If he'd only led the others farther up the hillside through the brush instead of across the upper end of the hay meadow, they wouldn't have encountered TT's forces at all. They'd have passed in the darkness without any trouble. And his plan for scattering the TT forces would have gone off as scheduled.

A little miscalculation like that had thrown the whole thing off. Now all he could do was salvage what he could. And get away with a whole skin.

He left his horse while he was still a quarter mile out in the hayfield. He took saddle and bridle off and turned the animal loose. He knew he was taking an enormous chance but he also knew that, riding the worn-out animal, he wouldn't get ten miles before pursuit caught up with him.

The horse trotted away, then stopped to graze. Carrying the saddle, Kiowa went on as silently and carefully as a stalking Indian brave.

Reaching the fence, he put the saddle and bridle carefully on the ground. He stood there like a shadow, waiting, listening.

For a long time he heard nothing but the restless stamping of the horses ground-tied outside the kitchen door. With the infinite patience of his nomadic plains ancestors, he continued to wait.

At last he heard the kitchen door. He heard the horses as the men caught and mounted them. He heard Johnny say, "Let's go, Sam."

He saw one ride south, another west. Johnny and Sam and another man passed him less than a hundred feet away, rode through an open gate, then north into the hayfield.

Kiowa waited until they were out of sight and hearing. Then he picked up his gear and made his way across the yard to the corral.

He was alone here at TT and he had lots of time. Johnny and his two companions had more than a mile to go before they even reached the oak-brush clump. They'd be riding slowly and cautiously. And even if they came right back, they'd be gone between half an hour and an hour, which would give him plenty of time.

He selected the best horse in the corral, caught and bridled him and led him out through the gate. He saddled the animal, then led him across the yard to the house.

Standing there, he wondered where the ranch office was. Somewhere off the big living room he supposed. That woman of Johnny's was probably in the kitchen, judging from the fact that the five had come from there. He'd make her put up some food for him. Maybe if she was pretty enough —

He faintly shook his head. There wasn't time for that.

He led the horse to the wire fence, looped the reins around the top wire. Then he retraced his steps to the kitchen door.

He opened the door suddenly and stepped inside, closing it quickly behind him. His gun was in his hand, the hammer back.

He didn't know what he had expected Johnny's wife to be. Older, certainly. Heavier probably. Johnny Toothaker was no kid and it startled Kiowa that he could have gotten a beauty like this one for a wife. She couldn't have been more than twenty-two or three, he judged.

She whirled as he came in the door, startled but not obviously afraid. He said, "Stand easy, sis. Just stand easy and you'll be all right."

Her fear appeared at the sound of his voice and that was almost as startling to him as his appearance had been to her. He'd never known the mere sound of his voice to inspire such fear before.

Her eyes widened and her face turned a ghastly shade of white. Her whole body began to tremble violently. Frozen she stood and for a moment he didn't know whether she was going to faint or run.

He said, "Whoa now! I don't know you. Or do I?"

She tried to speak and failed. But her eyes gave him the answer to his question. She did know him. She knew his voice. And that had to explain her fear.

He said harshly, "Where?"

She collapsed into a chair and buried her face in her hands. Her body continued to shake. Kiowa repeated harshly, "Where?"

Now she shook her head. He said, "You're a liar. You know me from someplace. Where?"

She shook her head again. He crossed the room, suddenly angry, and cuffed her. "You little bitch, say something!"

She did not reply. He holstered his gun and yanked her to her feet. He said, "I got ways of makin' women talk."

Her eyes watched him the way those of a rabbit watch a snake. He pulled her roughly against him. His hand slid down her back.

She struggled violently, but he held her inflexibly. "Where?"

"Denver." Her voice was the merest whisper and scarcely audible.

"When?"

"Two years – "

Scowling, he flung her away from him. She fell on the floor, her eyes closed tightly.

Kiowa's scowl faded and he began to smile. The smile grew wider and wider and at last a chuckle was born in his throat. That grew too and soon he was laughing.

His face turned red. He laughed until his breath was gone, then sank into a chair and gasped, "God!" he choked. "God! So you're that one! And married to the high and mighty Johnny Toothaker. Did you tell him about Kiowa and Whitey Post? Did you tell him before you married him that you'd been used before?"

Her eyes opened and for an instant there was less fear in them. Hate, burning and deadly.

He began to chuckle again. "Sometime I'll have to tell Johnny Toothaker all about his wife. I'll tell him how you amused Whitey and me the time we went over there on a bust. Only I won't tell him you fought, girlie. I'll tell him you liked every bit of it."

The hate didn't fade in her eyes but the fear returned.

Kiowa grinned evilly. "Don't like the idea of that, do you? All right. Maybe I won't tell Johnny about his wife. Depends on how hard you try to do what you're told to do."

Her voice was thin and filled with terror. She choked halfway through her question, had to swallow and start again. "What do you want?"

"Money will do to start. Where's the ranch office?"

Her glance switched to the door. Kiowa picked up a lamp and said, "Lead off, sis. And don't do anything you'll be sorry for."

She stood frozen, immobile. Kiowa seized her arm and yanked her across the room. He shoved her through the door.

She crossed the dining room, the living room, and went along a hall. She opened a door off that, and Kiowa pushed her inside.

He set the lamp down. "Where do they keep the money?"

She didn't reply, but her eyes answered for him. She glanced toward the floor beneath a table on the far side of the room. Kiowa crossed it, stooped and yanked out a metal strong box. He put it on the top of the table.

There was no lock on it. He lifted the lid.

Papers. Nothing but papers on top. He pulled them out and found a sheaf of bills beneath and a smaller box containing an assortment of coins, some of them gold.

No way of telling how much. But enough at least to keep him in grub, ammunition and fresh horses until he got clear away.

He stuffed it into his pockets. He turned and grinned at her. "That was quick. Maybe we still got time for a little fun before your gray-haired husband gets here."

Her eyes dilated with sheer terror. She turned and fled like a startled deer.

Kiowa seized the lamp and followed. He caught her at the end of the hall, seizing her by the collar of her blouse. It ripped. He released it and seized her arm.

He was laughing softly. "Maybe I'll just take you with me, sis." He was staring steadily at her shoulder, bared by the torn blouse. She pulled the blouse up hastily to cover it.

"Please! Please — "

"Get back in the kitchen and get me some grub."

She nodded frantically, turned and went to the kitchen, with Kiowa close behind.

Leaning against the doorjamb, he grinned at her. Her hands were shaking so violently she dropped almost everything she touched. She kept trying to pull the torn blouse up over her shoulder, but it wouldn't stay. And she needed her hands for what she was doing.

Eventually she got a floursack partly filled with food. Kiowa said, "That's enough! Come on. Maybe Johnny Toothaker won't be so damn reckless about followin' me if he knows I've got his precious wife. Besides, you'll be company nights crossing the mountains. A man's bed sure as hell gets cold."

"No! Please — "

Kiowa's grin disappeared. "Move, you little bitch! Before I spoil your pretty face."

He saw rebellion flare in her eyes. He reached for the lamp. An idea had just occurred to him and he wondered why he hadn't thought of it before. A blazing ranchhouse would delay pursuit better than anything else he could do. If it was well started before they got there, they'd probably assume Johnny's wife was trapped inside. By the time they discovered she wasn't, Kiowa would be safely away with her. And he'd have a hostage to bargain with if anything went wrong.

Besides, right now he wanted to hurt Johnny Toothaker. And this was the way that he could hurt him most.

Chapter Fifteen

Johnny slid his horse to a lunging halt outside the kitchen door. He saw no horses in the yard; there seemed to be nothing amiss with the house. And yet there was something – some primeval sense as old as time itself which made the skin on the back of his neck crawl with warning.

Kiowa was here. Johnny knew that more surely than he had ever known anything before. His feet hit the ground and he began to run, directly toward the door.

Kiowa might be waiting for him; he was fully aware of that. The outlaw might be standing inside the door, gun in hand, hammer thumbed back, ready to shoot the instant Johnny entered. He could hardly have failed to hear Johnny ride into the yard.

The realization didn't slow Johnny's running feet. Nor did his wounded leg, his weakness, slow him down. Right now his body was geared to its maximum effort, its maximum strength. Later he might collapse because of what he was doing now. But not until it was over. Not until Kiowa was dead.

He didn't open the door. He kicked it wide. He plunged inside, gun in hand.

He saw Robin first, shoulder bare, blouse torn. With fury-reddened eyes he swung his head, to glare at Kiowa standing across the room.

Kiowa held the lamp in his hand drawn back to throw. Johnny snapped a shot at him, knew it missed before the hammer even fell.

Kiowa threw the lamp and Johnny flung himself aside just as it left his hand.

He heard Robin scream. Kiowa's draw was like the darting tongue of a snake. The lamp was still in midflight across the room when Kiowa's gun appeared in his hand.

The man's gun belched smoke and flame the smallest part of a second before the thrown lamp struck. And Johnny was rolling on the floor beside the open door.

Robin screamed as the lamp shattered. A smell of kerosene filled the air and a tongue of flame licked along the floor. Johnny was trying to bring his gun to bear, hampered by his own rolling motion and the position he was in. But he was still unhurt. Kiowa's lightning shot had missed.

The light was bad right now. There was only the flickering glow from the flame licking at the spilled kerosene along the floor. It was growing though, and lighted Johnny's rolling form much better than it did Kiowa, half crouched on the other side of the room.

A table separated them, perhaps saving Johnny's life. For in the instant it was between them, Robin threw herself at the outlaw.

Johnny heard the man's savage curse, heard the blow he struck Robin. Then he was beyond the table and his gun was coming up –

Only Kiowa was no longer there. With the door into the dining room at his back, he had retreated through it and disappeared.

Robin lay hurt and whimpering on the kitchen floor. Johnny leaped to his feet and started after Kiowa.

And then he stopped. It would take but an instant to smother the flames. If he didn't smother them, by the time he returned the house would be beyond saving. Besides, there was Robin –

He seized a bucket of water from the stove. Whirling, he scattered it from one end of the blaze to the other with a single movement. The fire hissed, but it all went out, leaving the kitchen choked with steam and smoke.

Johnny groped across the room and found another lamp. He thumbed a match alight, raised the chimney and lighted it. He put it down and reached Robin, who was just getting up, in a couple of strides. They both spoke together, "Are you all right?"

For an instant their eyes locked desperately. Then, as both realized they had spoken the same words in unison, they began to laugh. There was a hysterical quality to their laughter, and it was soon over.

Johnny said, "You're really all right? He didn't hurt you?"

"No Johnny. I'm all right."

"I'll get after him then."

"Johnny, wait – " She stopped speaking suddenly. Johnny heard the drum of hoofs crossing the hard-packed yard, the hoofs of a single horse. They diminished rapidly and then disappeared altogether.

Robin said, "He made me take him into the office. He took all the money out of the cash box. Johnny, I'm sorry."

"About the money? Hell, I don't care about that. But the man's a mad dog." His mind was trying to decide which direction Kiowa had gone, but because of the baffling effect of the walls, he couldn't tell. He'd have to track.

He snatched a lantern from a hook by the back door. He lighted it and trimmed it. Robin cried, "Johnny, you're not well enough! You shouldn't – "

"Nobody else is here. And that's the man behind this whole stinking mess tonight. If it wasn't for him, Jake would still be alive. I'm not going to let him get away if I have to crawl after him."

He wondered where Sam and Dave were. He couldn't even remember whether he'd fired those three shots they'd agreed on, but he didn't think he had.

He fired them now into the air, then reloaded quickly. He jammed the revolver back into its holster, picked up the lantern and began to quarter back and forth across the yard.

A thousand tracks, most of them deeply indented by horses being ridden hard. Disgustedly, he put the lantern down. He'd have to guess and his first guess was that Kiowa had headed back to where he'd left his companions.

He swung astride and wheeled the horse toward the north meadow. Looking back, he saw Robin standing uncertainly in the doorway.

It had taken nerve to throw herself at Kiowa that way. It took nerve for her to stay alone in the house after what had happened only minutes before.

Tomorrow, as many tomorrows as he had, he would let her know what having her meant to him. He would never let her down again.

Darkness swallowed him. He thought he heard Sam and Dave go pounding past half a mile to the east, but he couldn't be sure. He yelled, got no answer, and so went on.

Hard, toward the scrub-oak clump in the middle of the field. He didn't figure he'd have to face them all. He guessed the ranchers had already quit, that the other three knew the game was up. Else Kiowa would not have come to the house alone. He would not have been interested in the few hundred dollars in the ranch strong box.

He meant to run, that was pretty plain. He meant to escape if he could the hangman's noose awaiting him for McRae's death, for the deaths of Nate and his boy.

Perhaps he had intended to run by himself with the money from the strongbox. Johnny thought he probably had. But Johnny's sudden appearance and Kiowa's failure to kill him had probably changed the man's mind. Now he needed Whitey and Lou.

Johnny gouged his horse savagely with his spurs, leaning low over the animal's neck. The horse jumped a ditch in the darkness, landing on the far side with a jolt that shook Johnny and sent shafts of pain from his hurt leg all the way through his body.

He clung to the saddle horn. The world seemed to reel. He crouched lower and hung on hard. Another jump like that last one – another jolt like that – and he'd be lying unconscious on the ground.

He shook his head, trying to clear it. He failed. The exertion of the night was catching up with him. Loss of blood from Doc's lancing the pitchfork wound had begun it, and the beating had furthered it. All this riding had taken what little strength remained in him.

He cursed savagely, bitterly. He wanted Kiowa. He wanted Whitey Post and Lou Saks. He wanted them to go to trial and hang for the murders they had committed tonight.

He raised his gun with his last waning strength and fired three times. He tried to yank his running horse to a halt.

The animal pulled up and this was the roughest gait of all to ride. Stopping, the horse made half a dozen stiff-legged, jolting leaps.

Johnny felt himself leave the saddle. He felt himself fall through empty air and felt the stunning impact as he struck the ground. He hoped, with his fading consciousness, that both his feet had slipped free of the stirrups, but he never really knew whether they had or not. Because the curtain of unconsciousness descended over his mind like a shroud. There was only utter silence and complete darkness.

Half stunned herself with shock, Robin watched Johnny quartering across the yard with the lantern and saw him ride out. Only when he had disappeared from her sight did she succeed in forcing herself to move.

She knew he should not be riding. She understood even better than Johnny did how weak he was. When he rose from the floor after Kiowa flung the lamp and shot at him — his face in the light of the flames from the spilled and burning kerosene had been ghastly, drawn, holding a quality of desperation because he knew he could not give in to the weakness that was rapidly overtaking him.

She ran across the yard toward the corral. She snatched a rope from a peg on the corral fence and tried, in darkness, to shake it out. Her fingers seemed to be all thumbs. Her hands began to shake and hysteria stole over her.

She flung the rope to the ground, turned and ran back in the direction from which she had come. Running, holding up her skirts, she ran out into the north hayfield.

She tripped over a branch irrigation ditch in the darkness and sprawled to the ground. She began to weep, but she got up and went on, sobbing and panting for lack of breath.

She saw and heard the three shots Johnny fired a quarter mile ahead. She went on running until she could run no more, yet even now she did not stop but slowed to an uncertain, stumbling walk.

Behind her she heard Sam and Dave pounding along in the direction of the shots.

She stopped now, and listened. She drew air into her starving lungs and exhaled it several times before she could even raise her voice enough to call to them. When she did, her voice broke and seemed too weak to carry as far as it must.

But they heard, and veered toward her. They pulled to a plunging halt a few feet away and Robin screamed at them, "Help him! He shouldn't be out here at all. He's so weak — "

Sam said, "Go back to the house. We'll find him." He spun his horse and pounded away with Dave following close behind.

Robin collapsed. She lay on the ground, gasping for breath, shaking from head to foot.

It seemed forever that she lay there. It seemed impossible to her that she would ever be able to breathe normally again. At last, however, her breathing became less frantic and she stumbled to her feet. She walked in the direction Sam and Dave had gone.

She met them coming back. Sam was walking, leading Johnny's horse. Johnny was inert and limp, lying across the saddle, being steadied by Dave who walked beside the horse, leading his and Sam's mounts behind.

Sam stopped when he saw her. "He's all right, Robin. He's all right. Only weak from loss of blood and from that beating he took in town. We'll get him home and put him to bed. Doc's on his way up here anyway."

Robin felt hysteria coming over her again and controlled it angrily. Johnny needed her and she would not let him down.

Sam called, "Dave. Help Robin up on one of the horses."

"Sure. Come on, Mrs. Toothaker."

She walked past Sam, past the horse bearing Johnny's limp body. She let Dave boost her up to one of the horses he was leading.

The little cavalcade went on. Robin clutched the saddle horn with both hands. Slowly her strength, her composure, began to return.

She didn't know how badly TT had hurt the attacking forces, but TT had been hurt badly itself. Jake McRae dead, Peters badly hurt.

Now Johnny had collapsed.

How much farther was it going to go before it stopped?

Chapter Sixteen

Kiowa was furious as he left the house, both furious and balked. Nothing seemed to be going right tonight. Nothing. If he'd had another five minutes, to get Robin away and set the house ablaze – But no. Johnny Toothaker had to show up.

He raced across the yard to the fresh horse he'd stolen earlier. He untied the animal and swung to his back. Through the kitchen windows he could see the orange, flickering light of the flames, but he knew Johnny would easily bring them under control.

Had he been able to get Robin, he would have fled alone. Now things were different. He had no appreciable start and no hostage. Even if darkness hid his trail, it wasn't going to last much longer. It must be almost dawn.

He would need Whitey Post and Lou Saks, at least for a while. Their horses, not as fresh as his, would play out first. Left behind, they'd delay the pursuit by putting up a fight. Maybe long enough to permit him to go on and get away.

Damn! He'd almost gotten his hands on that TT herd and his share of it would have been more than ten thousand dollars. But there was no use regretting the loss of the cattle now. He had a fresh horse and he had the contents of the safe. It would have to be enough.

He headed back through the north hayfield, spurring his horse savagely. At least he had chosen a good animal. The horse ran willingly and fast.

After he had gone about a mile, he slowed to a walk. Johnny might be coming along behind. No use advertising his location by running his horse. Besides, if he was going to elude pursuit, he would have to use the horse wisely.

Alternately walking and trotting the horse, he finally reached the oak brush clump in the middle of the field.

He rode through it to the center without dismounting. A horse nickered greeting to Kiowa's horse and Kiowa slapped a hand over his own mount's nostrils before he could reply.

He heard a voice, that of Whitey Post. "Kiowa? That you?"

"It's me." He went on and swung down from his horse. It didn't surprise him in the least to see that Whitey Post and Lou Saks were alone. He asked, his voice harsh, "What happened?"

Whitey growled, "They just, by God, up and walked away. They turned their backs on us, walked to their horses and rode away."

"And you let 'em go?"

"What else could we do? You can't just shoot that many men in the back. Besides, they weren't no good to us. They wouldn't fight no more."

Kiowa grunted. What Whitey said was true. Men that have lost their will to fight are useless.

He glanced toward the east. There was a faint line of gray along the irregular ridge rising above the road. That was the beginning of dawn. Kiowa said, "You two got any ideas?"

Whitey said, "We can still get those cattle if we stampede 'em down the road. We can get them to the Left Fork by dawn."

Kiowa's voice held a touch of contempt. "You know better than that."

"Well, we ought to have something for all we've done. Christ — "

"I got something. I just cleaned out the strong box."

"How much?"

"I don't know. I haven't counted it yet."

Lou Saks spoke for the first time. "Maybe we could still get Johnny Toothaker."

Kiowa said, "You get him. I'm getting the hell out of the country."

"I can't do it alone."

"Then don't do it. Or wait until we get ten or fifteen miles away. Maybe we can lay an ambush."

"You think they'll follow us?"

"I know damned well they will."

"I wish — "

Kiowa uttered a single, obscene word. "Sure. You wish you'd never gotten into this. But you did. So cut out the beefing and get on your horse. What's the quickest way out of this country anyway?"

"Up the Cottonwood, I guess. Over Cottonwood Pass."

"Then let's get going. It's starting to get light."

The three swung to the backs of their horses. Lou said hesitantly, "You going to split what you got out of the strong box with us?"

Kiowa didn't reply.

Lou said, "Christ, we oughta get something.

I ain't even got the month's pay they gave me when I left. I ain't got much more than half of it. An' just because the cattle steal didn't come off is no reason — "

Kiowa said, "Shut up. You'll get what's coming to you."

Their horses milled a moment in the center of the oak-brush clump and finally Kiowa said irritably, "Go ahead and lead out, damn it. You know the trail."

"Sure. Sure." Lou reined his horse around and picked his way north through the oak-brush clump. When he reached the open field, he spurred his horse and galloping, crossed the field, to the road. He held his broken arm awkwardly against his body with the other arm. Even so, his face was twisted with pain.

More than anything Kiowa hated leaving like a dog with his tail tucked between his legs. Yet he knew what it was to be hunted like an animal and he knew he was going to be hunted like that again. Even if Johnny's wife didn't tell him what Kiowa and Whitey had done to her two years ago in that Denver alley, Johnny wasn't going to let up. Not with McRae dead and Peters badly hurt.

A man had to know when he was licked and Kiowa knew he was licked this time. Not that there wouldn't be other times. A man could slip back into a country when no one was expecting him and even a lot of scores.

Lou held his horse to a gallop for over a mile, then let him drop into a steady, jolting trot. After the horse had cooled, he again lifted him to a gallop, and after a while slowed down again.

This way, the miles fell steadily behind. Dawn streaked the sky in the east with violet and then with pink. As the trio passed Three Mile Corral, the sun poked its brilliant golden rim above the ridges to the east.

The two guarding the TT herd watched them pass from the corral half a mile below the road. It didn't matter that they were seen, Kiowa thought. TT was going to be following trail and not in doubt as to which way the three had gone.

From here on, the road wound along the bank of the Cottonwood, and at last, seven miles above Three Mile Corral, began its climb toward the pass above.

Clear of the brushy bottom, Kiowa looked back. The pursuit was coming all right and it looked like a larger group than he had figured TT could muster. It looked like there were almost ten men in the group.

But they were still a long, long ways behind

and Kiowa knew that a lot can happen on a chase.

The sun was shining in the windows when Johnny Toothaker finally awoke. His first consciousness was of pain — pain in his swollen thigh around the pitchfork wound, in his battered face and bruised body. Then, slowly, memory began to return and with it came a discouraging realization that he had failed. Kiowa had escaped in darkness when Johnny fell from his horse. He was now probably miles away and with him the other two. What the ranchers had done, Johnny didn't know but he doubted if they had fled the country with the three. Most of them had families and homes here in the valley of the Cottonwood, which they would certainly refuse to leave.

He turned his head and saw Robin sitting beside the bed. Her eyes were soft, compassionate, worried. "How do you feel?"

He grinned wryly. "I guess I'll live. Is everything all right?"

She nodded. "Nothing more has happened, if that's what you mean. Sam and Dave brought in the bodies of Nate Dunn and his boy a while ago. They found them somewhere out in the hayfield."

"The sheriff?"

"He said he was going out to round up the men that burned the haystacks last night."

"What about Kiowa and Whitey Post?"

"They got away. I think Sam is going after them."

He started to get up, but Robin put a hand on his arm. "Wait a minute, Johnny. There's something I've got to tell you."

His eyes rested on her face.

"Before I met you, before we were married — " She looked steadily at the floor and her hands clenched into fists. At last she raised her head and looked directly into his eyes, though he could see it was very hard for her to do. "I was walking home one night and two men grabbed me and dragged me into an alley." Color now began to seep into her face. Her voice was almost a cry. "I fought them, Johnny, but it didn't do any good."

Johnny asked harshly, "Why are you telling me this now?"

"One of then was named Kiowa. I heard the other one say that name. And when Kiowa came here tonight, I recognized his voice."

"Does he know?"

She nodded. "I was so afraid when I heard his voice — he made me tell him why I was so afraid. And he said if he ever saw you he'd tell you I went with him because I wanted to.

That's why I'm telling you, Johnny."

Johnny muttered, "The son-of-a-bitch!"

"You don't believe – "

"That story? Hell no, I don't. If he opens his mouth to me about it I'll close it for good!"

Surprisingly, there was no jealousy in him because of what she had told him, no resentment because she had not told him before. There was only towering fury directed at Kiowa.

He looked into her face. His own softened and his arms went out and pulled her close to him. She buried her face in his chest and sobbed. When she pulled away there was something in her eyes – he couldn't have put a name to it but it made him feel ten feet tall.

He swung his feet over the side of the bed. "I'm going with Sam."

"You're not strong enough."

"I'm strong enough. Kiowa and Whitey Post are mine."

She reluctantly brought his clothes and he put them on, ignoring the darts of pain each movement caused. When he had finished he went to the kitchen, where Robin poured him a steaming mug of black coffee. He gulped it as quickly as he could.

Between gulps he asked, "How's Peters?"

"Conscious. He ate a good breakfast and demanded to be allowed to get up." She smiled wanly. "I didn't let him."

Johnny nodded. The door opened and Sam came in. Johnny said, "I'm going, Sam. Have someone saddle a horse for me."

"The hell you are. You handle the big jobs and I'll take care of the little chores like this one."

Johnny said, "That breed is mine. And Whitey is too."

Sam said, "No. It's going to be a damn hard chase and you're not strong enough. You've lost too much blood."

"Do I have to fight you, Sam?" The tone was bantering but the look in Johnny's eyes was not.

Sam stared at him steadily for several moments. At last he shrugged. "All right Johnny. It's your funeral."

"Don't be so cheerful. Now tell someone to saddle me a horse while I finish this coffee."

Sam went out and Johnny gulped the last of the coffee.

Robin asked, "You're not going just because of what I told you?"

He said, "I was going anyway. Those three shot Peters and killed Jake. Kiowa killed

Nate and Will Dunn. I've got plenty of reasons for wanting them. I'd have gone even if you hadn't told me."

She looked relieved but still worried. "Be careful, Johnny. I want you back." She tried to smile but it wasn't very successful. "I'm awfully fond of you."

He kissed her, held her away and looked at her. "You'll be all right. Most of the crew will be staying here."

"I'm not afraid." But the words were not as sure as they might have been. She was afraid.

He went outside. Sam was already mounted and waiting. So were Dave Dunklee, Jess, Luke and Frank. Sam held the reins of the horse that had been saddled for Johnny to ride.

He took the reins from Sam's hand and swung up. He hit the saddle hard and hurt his wounded leg, but his face didn't change. Anticipating his question, Sam said, "There'll be four men here to look after things."

Johnny nodded. Sam led out east up the narrow lane and Johnny followed. He supposed Sam had already scouted around enough to determine the direction the fleeing trio had gone.

Over Cottonwood Pass. He knew that immediately from the direction of the trail. A long ride lay ahead. He turned and lifted a hand to wave at Robin, standing in the yard.

The night had been incredibly long. It seemed impossible that so many things had happened since yesterday afternoon.

Up the road they went with Sam riding in the lead, carefully watching the ground for trail. Sweeping along at a fast trot, they raised a cloud of dust behind.

Past the Brush Creek forks, past Three Mile Corrall. And now at last, Sam pulled to a halt to briefly rest his horse. He looked at Johnny as he said, "We may not get 'em after all. Looks like seven or eight of our neighbors got after them first."

Chapter Seventeen

After leaving the Cottonwood, the trail began to climb steeply, zigzagging across the brushy face of the first tall peak like a series of awkward "z's" drawn there by a gigantic child. It was tall brush here, sagebrush, oak-brush, service-berry brush, but at this point the trail was still wide and clear, pounded flat by the hoofs of a thousand cattle driven over it less than two days before.

Here it was that the horses of Whitey Post and Lou Saks first showed signs of giving out. Their upward climbing steps became sluggish and reluctant and they stopped often to blow.

Lou's horse, rented from the livery barn in town, hadn't been much to begin with. Whitey's mount, though a good enough animal, was tired from the long ride yesterday between the

San Paulo range and town, further tired by the long night of riding. Neither horse would last to the top of the pass.

Kiowa began to look ahead, searching for a suitable spot to stop. It had to be a place from which they could command an unobstructed view of the trail behind. It had to provide cover for both horses and men and it had to turn up soon.

Because the pursuit was gaining at a rate equal to that the fleeing three maintained. And maybe four miles behind. That meant by the time Kiowa and his two companions had traveled another four miles the pursuit would have come within shooting range.

He hipped around in his saddle and stared back, his eyes cold, brooding, angry. It wasn't TT following. He'd guessed that when he first glimpsed the pursuit and he verified his first guess now. It was the ranchers who had been their allies the night before.

But Toothaker and Tolle and their men would be coming too. Ah Good, he thought, the time is getting short.

A peculiar certainty touched him and left a coldness in his spine. This was one time he wasn't going to escape. This time he wasn't going to get away.

He swung his head and gazed at the backs

of the pair ahead of him. He stared at the sweaty rumps and heaving sides of the horses they rode. He glanced down at his own mount, breathing deeply, strongly, steadily.

What the hell was the matter with him this morning, anyway? Everything was in his favor now despite the way things had turned out last night. There was no reason why he shouldn't get away. His horse was strong; he had money to buy another on the far side of Cottonwood Pass.

Four more miles and Whitey and Lou would have to make a stand because they'd have no choice. Let them think he was going to stay with them. When their attention was engaged, he'd get his chance to slip away.

But he needed the right spot before he could risk a stop. And suddenly he saw it about a mile ahead.

They had left the brush. They had passed through a heavy fringe of timber that guarded the rocky slopes beyond. They had skirted the side of one bare, gray granite peak.

Now they were approaching another, even bleaker than the last. The trail was practically gone because it was now too high for regular travel either by cattle or men. It rose steadily, scarcely discernible in spots because of the crushed slide rock that had tumbled down to cover it.

Like a thread laid across the cold, bleak face of this mountain land, it crossed the side of the mountain they approached, angled upward and dropped off suddenly on the other side, at the start of a narrow saddle between the two towering mountain peaks.

It was Kiowa's spot. He knew it the instant he saw it. There was timber on the far side of the saddle to conceal him briefly when he left. There were deep, rocky gulches on both sides of the saddle, gulches choked with down timber and brush, gulches a man and horse simply could not cross.

He said, "We'll stop the other side of that saddle. We can hold 'em until the horses are rested up."

Neither man answered him. But they studied the saddle as carefully as he.

Glancing back again, he knew they had reached it none too soon. For suddenly the sharp crack of a rifle came thinly on the cold mountain air, to be echoed back and forth from peak to peak until it was finally lost. In spite of the impossible range of it, Whitey spurred his lagging horse.

The animal stumbled. Kiowa snarled, "You goddam fool! Be careful, unless you want to walk!"

They ceased to climb across the granite peak. The trail leveled out, then headed downward slightly toward the narrow saddle between the peaks.

Kiowa's glance traveled to right and left. There was a hitch in his plan. There was always a hitch. The gulches, at least the one on the left, did not remain impassable for more than a couple of miles. Down there two or three miles away the left one leveled out and provided a way across.

So the element of time now entered in. The time it took men to travel that two and a half miles and back.

Sliding, trembling, drenched with sweat, the horses of Whitey and Lou descended to the relatively level spine of the saddle itself. Kiowa followed, the uneasiness he had earlier felt increasing now.

They crossed quickly, dismounted with relief in the timber on the far side. Whitey and Lou tied their horses just within its protective shelter, but Kiowa went a little farther on before he tied his horse to a tree. He walked back to find Whitey and Lou crouched behind a rock, their rifles stuck out in front of them.

He said, "Hold your fire until they get in range. So far they don't even know we've stopped."

"Think we can hold 'em till dark?" This was

Whitey's thick voice, made more so by the fact that breathing the cold, thin air through his mouth hurt his ragged gums.

Kiowa shook his head. "No. They'll get behind us long before dark. But we've got a while. Maybe long enough to rest the horses so they'll make it to the top and down the other side."

He crouched beside the pair. His eyes were steady, black, cold and without expression. He watched the pursuing riders draw closer.

He counted seven now. They rode slowly, steadily, without hurrying. They rode like men who know they will succeed, who intend to succeed no matter how long it takes.

He was conscious of the mounting odds. Before long, Johnny Toothaker, Sam Tolle and whatever crewmen they had brought along would be arriving on the scene.

He laid his rifle on the rock in front of him and sighted carefully. He waited until he had a good, clear bead on the man leading the pursuit. Then he fired.

Smoke puffed from his rifle, momentarily obscuring his view. Up there on the hillside a horse fell, kicking. His rider scrambled clear and stood up.

Kiowa cursed softly to himself. He'd drawn his bead squarely but either the range or the wind had fooled him. The bullet had dropped two feet or more.

Whitey and Lou had opened fire now. Bullets kicked up rock dust up there wherever they struck. Kiowa said, "Hold it. That's enough."

Whitey growled, "Hell, we might—"

"Yeah. You might hit something. You might run out of shells, too."

He saw the man he had put afoot pointing off to the right. He saw three of the pursuers detach themselves from the others and ride in that direction. They had gone to cross the gulch and come upon the fleeing trio from behind.

Now the remaining four retired, two of them riding one horse. They disappeared behind the rocky granite peak, but reappeared ten or fifteen minutes later, sheltered by a shoulder of rock and several hundred yards closer than they had been before. Their rifles began to crack spitefully, and bullets struck the rocks behind which Kiowa and the others crouched, scattering razor-sharp splinters and then whining off into the distance.

This continued for nearly ten minutes. Ten minutes during which those three circling in from behind came closer. Kiowa scowled. How long would it take them to cover those five or six rough and rock-strewn miles? Under normal circumstances, at normal altitude, their horses could probably cover it in fifteen minutes with ease.

Here, however, where the going was hard, it would take double that length of time.

Which didn't give Kiowa much time to spare. He began to ease back away from the shelter of the rock. The barrage above intensified.

He grunted, "I'm going back and bushwhack the three coming up behind. That'll give us a little more time."

Whitey grunted, "Good idea." Lou just stared at Kiowa with scared eyes and a white face and tried to burrow lower behind his rock.

Kiowa got up and sprinted for the timber where they had left the horses. He had no intention of bushwhacking anybody. If he got his horse and rode away it was going to be an hour or more before anybody even knew that he was gone. By that time—

He reached the shelter of the timber. Whitey's and Lou's horses were stamping and tugging at their reins, frightened by the echoing rifle shots. Neither was hurt, but they ought to be tied farther back. Not that it mattered, because neither Whitey nor Lou would use them again.

He went on, heading for the place he had tied

his own horse. And then he stopped. He stared in shocked unbelief. *His horse was down.*

He broke into a run, unable to believe his eyes. He stared down at the animal, at the scarlet stain on the brown carpet of pine needles.

A ricocheting bullet had cut his horse's throat. Somehow it had found its way through the screen of timber, and by freakish mischance had struck his horse squarely in the neck.

Even now, the horse was wheezing its last, dying breaths. Its sides heaved spasmodically a couple of times and then were still. The horse's open eyes lost their shine and began to dull.

Kiowa's mind was sick. His chest felt hollow. His heart thumped like a drum.

Something began to flood his mind like a dark and rising tide. Hate. The most burning, violent hate he had even known. His chance to escape was gone. But perhaps his chance for revenge was not.

He turned and looked back in the direction from which he had come. No use taking Whitey's or Lou's horse. They wouldn't go ten miles, or even five.

Kiowa backed away, instinctively, into thicker timber. Both hatred and anger were growing in him like a fire fanned by a stiff wind.

Jesus! Nothing had gone right since he'd tangled with Toothaker and Tolle. Nothing. He'd never seen anything quite like it. It was as though— he shivered involuntarily and scowled because he did. There was nothing supernatural about it. It was just chance. Luck.

Maybe so. He was going to find out and break that luck. Lacking a fresh horse, he could not go on. Nor could he stay here and fight it out with seven men against him. But one course remained. Go back. Go back down the Cottonwood afoot.

Beyond that, he didn't plan. But there was a need in him that couldn't be denied. He wanted to hurt Toothaker and Tolle and thus get even. He particularly wanted to hurt Johnny Toothaker.

A strong streak of superstition ran through Kiowa, this probably being inherited from his Indian forebears. And in the back of his mind was the unformed thought that before his luck could change, Johnny Toothaker had to die.

He heard, distantly, the crack of a dead limb. He waited no longer, but turned and silently made his way along parallel to the gulch and away from the sound. After he had gone a quarter mile, he picked his way to the edge of the gulch and looked across.

The men on the hillside were still firing at Whitey and Lou. The three who had come up behind had not yet showed themselves.

A horse couldn't make it across the gulch but a man on foot could. Kiowa picked his way down the rocky slope, climbing over down timber and crawling through nearly impenetrable tangles of brush in a way no horse could ever do. Staying below the rim of the gulch, he traveled away from the sound of gunfire until it had faded almost altogether from his ears. Only then did he emerge.

From where he stood on the bald side of one of those towering mountain peaks, he could see fifty miles to the south, could see the valley of the Cottonwood for almost its entire length. He could even see the thread, of green that marked the fields of TT ranch.

The way was long by horseback trail. But a man on foot could cut the miles in half. And travel faster because he traveled downhill.

With a last glance behind, Kiowa began his long walk back, leaping from rock to rock with all the agility of a mountain goat. And as he traveled, he began to lose his sense of defeat, his frustrated sense of being trapped.

Johnny Toothaker was behind every bit of

bad luck that had happened to him and Johnny Toothaker was going to die. After that, perhaps many things would change.

Chapter Eighteen

The farther they traveled up the twisting road that now followed the brush-grown bed of the Cottonwood, the easier the trail became. The fleeing trio had apparently made no attempt to hide their tracks and the pursuing small ranchers' tracks, overlying theirs, made a trail it was impossible to miss.

From here on, it looked all cut and dried. Incensed by the cold-blooded murder of Nate Dunn and Will, the ranchers would, it appeared, catch them first and do what Sam and Johnny wanted to do. Shoot or hang the three.

Why, then, did this peculiar uneasy feeling linger in his mind? Why did quiet terror continue to grow in Johnny? Was it premonition that he would be killed or that Sam would be?

He wished he knew.

Nine miles above the Brush Creek forks the road became a narrow trail, left the bed of the Cottonwood and began to climb in zigzagging switchbacks across the brush-grown face of a towering mountain to the east.

The air grew cooler with the increasing altitude as they climbed. And brush gave way to brooding dark spruce and pine, later to gold-flecked aspens with their pale white trunks.

Still the trail was cut and dried, easy to follow, impossible to lose. Growing no fresher but growing no older either. And always rising toward the distant peaks where the Cottonwood began in a glacial bed of ice, where nothing grew, where the land was all gray rock and cold white snow and ice.

At first the gunfire was so faint as to seem imagined, but as they went on, it occasionally came sharp and clear and unmistakable on a shifting drift of wind.

Johnny grinned at Sam. "They've treed 'em," and Sam nodded.

But Johnny's grin did not long remain on his drawn and weary face. That strange uneasiness was eating at him again.

He tried to reason it away. He knew that Kiowa and the other two were ahead. There could be no doubt. The trail was plainly written on the ground.

He knew something else. The ranchers had caught the three and made them stop. They might even have surrounded them.

Hell it couldn't be more cut and dried. Before nightfall all three of the outlaws would be dead, strapped across their saddles and on their way to town.

He killed his uneasiness forcibly. He was getting to be a regular old woman.

On and on they went, ever upward, and now the sounds of gunfire were plainer, clearer. Then suddenly the gunfire stopped.

Sam spurred his horse ahead with Johnny and the others following suit. They thundered across a bare gray hillside and then could look down upon the narrow saddle ahead.

Nothing moved. Touched by sudden concern, Johnny spurred his horse, ignoring Sam's warning shout, "Wait, you damn fool! You want to get killed?"

But no shots cracked out in the thin, high air. No sound broke the stillness save for the echo of Sam's shout and the metallic ringing of shod hoofs against the granite rubble underfoot.

Down Johnny went and crossed the saddle at a run. He swung to the ground on the other side, his gun in hand.

Whitey Post was sprawled forward over the

rock he had been crouching behind. Apparently he had tried to rise and had collapsed forward. There was a small hole in the center of his forehead.

Lou Saks, lacking Whitey's courage, had apparently tried to run. He was sprawled face downward on the ground fifteen or twenty yards behind the group of rocks and Whitey Post.

Johnny's uneasiness was back, stronger than before, with justification now. Kiowa's body was not in sight and somehow Johnny knew even as he sprinted into the timber that it was not here. Kiowa had escaped.

He passed the tied horses of Whitey and Lou. He ran beyond, and pulled to a sudden halt beside the body of the TT horse Kiowa had ridden here.

The blood pool that had formed beneath the horse's throat was brown and dry. Johnny holstered his gun with a scowl.

Kiowa was afoot unless he had managed to get one of the pursuers' horses away from them.

Johnny's scowl deepened. He doubted if Kiowa would have been willing to risk going on unless his horse was fresher than those of the men pursuing him. Therefore, when his horse was killed, he had probably gone someplace afoot.

But where? On toward the far side of Cottonwood Pass? Johnny shook his head. The pursuing ranchers would catch him inevitably if he did that and Kiowa was smart enough to know it.

Back then. Back into the valley of the Cottonwood, as angry and vengeful as a rattler someone has been prodding with a stick. Desperate, knowing that his chance of escape was very slim.

He circled the dead horse, staring closely at the ground. He found a single track, nothing after that. The pine needles were like a cushion, revealing a footprint only seconds after it was made, then springing back. Beyond the timber and the carpet of pine needles— Johnny broke into a trot, stopping only when he saw what the footing was in the open. Rock. Slide rock, crushed by the grinding of snow and ice and a million years of time. It wouldn't even hold a running horse's track.

Beyond, the gulch to the south and more granite rock. To the north more timber, more cushiony beds of pine needles and leaves.

Where the ranchers had gone, Johnny didn't know. He doubted if they had gone on north, for to do so would be to abandon their homes and families. No. They were probably waiting deep in the timber until Johnny and Sam went back. They they'd go back too, still anonymous, but with their vengeance achieved.

Johnny returned to his horse, running. Sam and the others were just now picking their way across the narrow, rocky saddle. Johnny swung to his horse's back, spurred to meet them.

Sam asked, "All three?"

Johnny shook his head. "Just two. Kiowa's disappeared. You stick around up here a while and see if you can pick up his trail. I'm going back."

"You think—"

"I don't know what the hell to think. He's afoot. He might figure going back was safer than going on."

He didn't wait for Sam to agree. He dug spurs into his horse's ribs and pounded across the saddle and back south along the trail.

He understood why he'd felt uneasy now. Some reasoning process he didn't comprehend himself had told him Kiowa might come back. He stared ahead, down into the valley and beyond. How long would it take a man afoot to slide and walk and run to the bottom of the valley? Less than it took a man and horse to make it over the trail. Yet Johnny didn't leave his horse because with his leg wounded, as weak as he was, he'd make it faster if he kept his horse. Afoot he might not make it at all.

He spurred recklessly, urging the horse to speeds that upset the animal's gait. Only at long intervals did he rest the horse and when he did the horse stood trembling until Johnny urged him on again.

Back across the rocky faces of the mountains above timberline. Down through the fragrant pines and golden quaking aspen, across the brushy faces of the lower peaks until at last he zigzagged down the last steep pitch of trail and reached the road winding along the banks of the Cottonwood.

He spurred the horse into a gallop and held him to it as long as he dared. Ration the horse's strength, he thought. Kill him if necessary, but don't risk killing him too soon.

He swung in at Three Mile Corral and changed saddle and bridle from his heaving mount to a fresh horse there. Then, riding as fast as the horse could run, he pounded again on down the road.

As he traveled, the sun had gradually sunk from its place halfway up the western sky to the horizon far below. Now it was setting, sinking behind the ridges to the west, dyeing the high, puffy clouds a brilliant copper-gold. As Johnny brought the house in sight the color faded from the clouds, leaving the land blanketed in soft, gray dusk.

And he heaved a slow, involuntary sigh of relief. The house at TT looked exactly as it always had. Smoke rose from the kitchen chimney. It seemed to slumber there, untouched.

Feeling a bit foolish, Johnny slowed his horse. Then, as uneasiness crept back over him, he urged him to a gallop again. Maybe he'd been wrong. But until he was sure, until he had reached the place and seen for himself, he'd keep going just as he had all day.

On down the road he went and turned in at the lane leading to the house.

Dusk had deepened quickly in the last few minutes until now it was almost dark. Yet no lamps winked on in the house. Nothing stirred in the yard. The bunkhouse remained silent and dark.

A warning sense stirred in Johnny's mind. Instead of pulling up immediately before the house, he galloped past it to the bunkhouse. Only when he had reached its shelter did he dismount.

A new kind of terror possessed him. He was certain that Kiowa was here. But where was the crew? Where was Robin? Why was the place deserted?

He wanted to race across the yard and burst into the house. It would have been the normal thing to do. Perhaps that was why he stubbornly held back.

Scowling, he peered at the house from the corner of the bunkhouse wall. Urgency prodded him until he quieted it with reason. He was wasting no time. If Kiowa were gone, even if he had taken Robin as a hostage, there was nothing Johnny could immediately do about it. Trying to follow trail in the darkness would be the worst kind of foolhardiness.

And if Kiowa and Robin were gone it was probable that the remaining members of the crew were already on their trail.

Yet some strange sense he did not himself understand told Johnny neither Kiowa nor Robin was gone. They were here, in the house, and Kiowa was waiting for Johnny to come bursting in.

Behind him he heard the scuff of a boot and whirled, drawing his gun and thumbing back the hammer as he did. From a ready half-crouch, he saw the dark bulk of an approaching man.

His finger rested lightly on the trigger of his gun. And then a familiar man's voice called, "Johnny? That you?"

Arleigh Peters' voice. Johnny eased the hammer of his gun down and holstered the gun. Peters materialized out of the darkness, hobbling painfully on a makeshift crutch. Johnny asked harshly, "What the hell's going on?"

"The bastard came back, Johnny. He walked in here about four-thirty this afternoon. He was in the house before we even knew he was around."

"Why the hell—" Johnny's voice was angry.

"The men couldn't help it, Johnny. They were outside, Robin ran 'em out. I was asleep. First I knew anything was wrong. Robin let out a yell. There was a scuffle. I got out of bed and snatched my gun—" He stopped and a kind of helplessness entered his voice. "He had her, Johnny. He held her between him and me and made me drop my gun. Then he made me get the hell out of the house. Told me to tell the crew if they weren't off the place in ten minutes he was going to kill her."

"He wouldn't—"

Peters sagged against the wall of the bunkhouse. His breath came in short, uneven gasps. "Maybe not," he said. "But it was a chance I couldn't take. Not with Robin's life."

Johnny said, "Thanks, Arleigh. You sit down before you fall down."

Peters slid to the ground, the bunkhouse wall at his back. He grunted painfully as he pushed his injured leg out straight.

Johnny asked, "What does he want?"

"You. He's waitin' for you in there and he doesn't intend to give you a chance. I figure he'll take off once he's got rid of you, keeping Robin with him to make sure nobody comes after him. It's the only chance he's got right now."

Johnny stared bleakly at the darkened house. Kiowa had beaten him after all. He couldn't risk Robin's life by arguing or trying to outwit the man. He'd have to walk in there and take his chances without putting up a fight.

The worst of it was, even if he did exactly what Kiowa demanded, he had no assurance that Robin would be safe. Certainly Kiowa would take her with him as a hostage to discourage pursuit. And once her usefulness to him was gone, he'd think nothing of killing her and leaving her body where it might never be found. Nor would he hesitate to mistreat her even if he didn't kill her.

Johnny's jaw clenched hard. He didn't have much time to make up his mind. Time was running out fast.

He had never felt more helpless. Kiowa held all the advantage and there was nothing Johnny could do but play into Kiowa's hand. He was going to have to walk into that darkened house like a condemned man walking to the gallows. Kiowa would shoot at him and Johnny didn't dare shoot back.

Peters asked, "What are you going to do?"

Johnny said, "What can I do? I'm going in and do exactly what he tells me to. But when he leaves, tell Sam and the others I said to follow him. Follow him if he goes a thousand miles. And if he hurts Robin I want him strung up by his thumbs."

Peters said softly, "Johnny, you can count on that."

Johnny stepped out into the darkened yard. Behind him he heard Peters breathe softly, "Good luck, Johnny. Good luck."

Slowly he began to pace across the yard toward the silent house, toward the sudden death he knew awaited him.

Chapter Nineteen

The distance across the yard seemed a thousand miles. It was dark, but not yet completely. The sky was just light enough to silhouette the bulk of the house and throw a small amount of illumination upon objects in the yard.

Apparently Kiowa saw Johnny coming, apparently was not willing to risk a shot in such uncertain light. Johnny stopped as though he had run into a wall when he heard Kiowa's shout from an upstairs window. "Toothaker? That you?"

"It's me." Johnny waited, motionless. His mind was racing, trying to find some loophole in the trap Kiowa had caught him in and unable to do so.

Kiowa yelled, "Stand right still and hear me out or you'll wish you had. I've got your wife."

Johnny neither answered nor moved.

Kiowa yelled, "You hear? I've got your wife up here. It's going to be up to you what I do with her."

Johnny's voice was choked with fury. "What do you want me to do?"

Kiowa laughed with harsh mockery. "Changed your goddam tune, ain't you?"

Johnny's fists clenched with the effort he made at controlling himself. Kiowa yelled, "You're trying to figure a way to get me before I can hurt her, ain't you? Don't waste your time. She'll be between me and you until you're dead." He laughed again. "She's fond of you, though I'm damned if I know why. She says that's why she's been so agreeable with me while we was waitin' for you." There was a suggestive tone in Kiowa's voice that made his meaning unmistakable.

Controlling himself, holding his body still, was the hardest thing Johnny had ever done. He wanted to charge across the yard and burst into the house. He wanted to take those stairs three at a time and reach the top with his gun roaring the way he wanted to roar right now himself.

Up there in the bedroom window, Kiowa was chuckling. But at last he yelled, "All right! Come on! Only keep it in mind. This woman of yours is going to be between you and me."

As though suddenly released, Johnny sprang ahead and sprinted across the yard. He took the steps to the porch in a bound and slammed the front door wide. And then, just inside the door, he stopped.

This was what Kiowa wanted; this was exactly what the man expected him to do. Slam in and charge upstairs, every movement announcing his location and direction and speed. While Kiowa waited in darkness, in silence.

Johnny backed suddenly and silently out the door. Avoiding a creaking board and walking as softly as a cat, he crossed the porch and went down the steps.

Hugging the wall of the house, he ran to the rear and silently entered the kitchen door. Here, just inside the door, he holstered his gun and stooped to remove his boots.

Still silently, he crossed the kitchen and from this direction entered the enormous living room.

He supposed Kiowa was still upstairs and he knew the risk he took by refusing to charge up there and let himself be killed.

He risked Robin's life. But he risked that no matter what he did. He had no guarantee that Kiowa would release her safely even after he had escaped and after Johnny was dead.

Let Kiowa, then, do the worrying for a while. Let him sweat while he wondered where Johnny was, what his intentions were. Johnny was taking a chance but he didn't think Kiowa would risk hurting Robin now for once he did she was no longer useful to him as a shield.

For what seemed an interminable length of time he waited motionless there in the center of the big front room, his head turned toward the stairs, his ears straining for sounds. Then he heard Kiowa's angry shout from the direction of the stairs, "Damn you Toothaker! You want me to kill her? Or should I just break her arm for a start?"

Johnny held his breath, tormented by indecision. The thought of Robin enduring pain like that at the hands of the outlaw was intolerable. Deliberately throwing away any advantage he might have gained by silent entry of the house, he shouted, "All right! I'm coming!"

He crossed the room to the foot of the stairs, gun in hand, making no effort now to be quiet but tensed and ready for the slightest movement or sound from above. He reached the foot of the stairs and began his climb.

Some half detached part of his mind counted the steps as he climbed. One. Two. Three. The fifth one creaked and instantly it did a muzzle flare blossomed above him at the head of the stairs.

Johnny tried to fling himself forward, but was much too late. He felt a bullet burn along his thigh, felt the instant rush of blood and staggered hard to the right against wall and bannister as the numbed leg gave way.

He felt utterly helpless and furious because he was. Kiowa could shoot at movements, at sounds, and if he sprayed enough lead down the stair-well he couldn't fail to hit Johnny eventually in a vital spot. Yet Johnny could do nothing — nothing but try blindly to reach the head of the stairs as quickly as he could.

He tried the hurt leg, found that it would bear his weight if he helped slightly by clinging to the oaken bannister at his side. Trying to be as quiet as possible, he resumed his climb.

The gun roared again up at the head of the stairs and this bullet showered Johnny with splinters as it tore into the steps immediately in front of him. Powdersmoke from Kiowa's gun was blinding and choking and despite his effort to control himself, Johnny began to cough.

The cough bent him forward and probably saved his life for Kiowa's third bullet burned along the muscles of his back like the light but red-hot touch of a branding iron.

Running, coughing, hurt and certain he would never reach the head of the stairs alive,

Johnny's mind still could work and did. He knew something had to drive Kiowa back from the head of the stairs if only for the briefest instant.

He thumbed back the hammer on his gun and fired, straight into the air over his head. Given time, Kiowa might rationalize and decide Johnny had fired only for effect, but there wasn't going to be time for rationalization. Johnny figured surprise and reflex would drive the outlaw back a step or two.

Apparently it did. Kiowa's gun was silent while Johnny took the remaining steps at a hard scrambling run.

He flung himself flat on the floor at the head of the stairs, hands extended before him, as Kiowa's last two shots ripped through the air where his body had been. The flares created light, enough for Robin to faintly see him on the floor, and she began to scream hysterically.

Johnny heard the sound of a blow, a hard and vicious one, and Robin's screaming stopped. She struggled as Kiowa retreated down the hall with her and Johnny heard the savage sounds of several more blows before her struggling ceased.

He was up, then, lunging along the hall in the direction the two had gone. By struggling, by screaming, by forcing him to knock her unconscious, Robin might well have saved Johnny's life. Tearing along the hall he heard the solid thump of a body striking the floor, and while the knowledge that she was hurt and unconscious further infuriated him, he knew that her courage had evened the odds, that now he had an equal chance.

To his right through an open door, he heard the rattle of empty shellcases on the floor as Kiowa punched them out. He skidded to a halt and whirled.

The flare of Kiowa's muzzle flash lighted the interior of the room and threw a shaft of light briefly through the door and against the wall opposite it. Then Johnny was in the doorway, trying to penetrate the inky darkness with his eyes, failing because there wasn't any light.

Crouched, ready, gun in hand and cocked, he waited squarely in the doorway. His breathing was regular, soft, deliberately kept so because he didn't want to give Kiowa anything at which to shoot.

Kiowa, similarly, stood silent and motionless inside the room, waiting for sound, for movement, for something that would betray Johnny's exact location to him.

It was Robin, stirring and groaning on the floor, who unwittingly provided the diversion Johnny so desperately needed. Stirring, she gave Johnny her location and Kiowa's too for the man unthinkingly took a step away from her.

Johnny fired, leaped aside out of the doorway instantly as he did. He immediately knew he had missed for Kiowa's gun roared like an echo.

The flash lighted the room for the briefest instant and died. But not before Johnny's eyes had photographed the scene – Kiowa standing crouched to one side of the window, Robin prone on the floor. His gun muzzle swung the slightest bit as his finger tightened on the trigger and let the hammer fall.

There was a new and different sound this time, coming so close on the heels of the report as to seem imagined, but Johnny knew exactly what it was. It was the sound of a soft-nosed bullet striking flesh. Another sound followed that, a louder, more solid sound as Kiowa drove back with a crash against the wall.

Pinned to the wall by the force of Johnny's hard-striking bullet, reflex triggered his gun and again the muzzle flare lighted up the room.

Kiowa's eyes were glazed; his mouth hung slack and loose. He was sliding down the wall but Johnny was too tight-strung to hold back just because another shot might not be needed now. He triggered almost as reflexively as

Kiowa had and again heard the solid strike of a bullet against human flesh.

Sound echoed and re-echoed thunderously through the house and died, leaving Johnny's ears ringing. He scarcely heard the thump as Kiowa's body hit the floor.

He was crossing the room, shoving his smoking gun into its holster, searching for Robin's body on the floor.

He found her and knelt, and gathered her up in his arms as though she were a child. He staggered out of the smoke-filled room and along the hall, yelling down the stairs as he reached their head, "Peters! Damn it, somebody light a lamp!"

They must have entered the house while the battle was going on, for there was stir and movement down there, and voices, and the flare of a match followed almost immediately by the light of a lamp.

Johnny carried Robin down the stairs and laid her on the huge, cowhide-covered sofa. He sat down on it beside her. Her eyes were open, watching him.

Scarcely more than twenty-four hours had passed since Johnny came riding into the yard to find Lou Saks pursuing Robin out of the bunkhouse door. Men had died and smoldering hatreds had been exposed, but at its end there was this, this enduring closeness that Johnny knew nothing could ever again threaten or destroy.

He saw the bruise on her cheek, the trickle of blood from one corner of her mouth. But when he asked, "Are you hurt?" she said indignantly, "Of course I'm not. But you are. Now let me up and let me bandage you before you bleed to death."

She sat up, got to her feet and crossed the room to find bandages for his wounds. He grinned at her, liking this feeling she gave him of standing ten feet tall. He felt complacent and maybe a little smug for he knew at last that a man whose woman makes him feel this way has no justification for jealousy. He settled back on the sofa, grinning almost foolishly, and waited impatiently for Robin to return.